p. 235-258

 na̅
mas

D1067814

ORPHAN PAUL

Orphan Paul

A Novel by

MAXIM GORKY

Translated by
LILY TURNER AND MARK O. STREVER

19   46

A PURSUIT PRESS BOOK

Boni and Gaer • New York

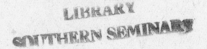
LIBRARY
SOUTHERN SEMINARY

All rights reserved

*Including the right of reproduction
in whole or in part in any form*

Copyright 1946 *by* PURSUIT PRESS, INC.

Published in cooperation with

BONI AND GAER, INC.

15 East 40th Street
New York 16, N. Y.

*Manufactured in the United States of America
by* PARISH PRESS, INC., *New York.*

A NOTE FROM THE PUBLISHER

About the Discovery of this Novel

Orphan Paul is the first novel Maxim Gorky wrote. It was written in 1894 when the author was only 26 years old and ran serially in a local paper of Nizhni Novgorod, since re-named Gorky in his honor.

Shortly before his death, Gorky took up the story again, evidently with the idea of including it in the definitive collection of his works. The original newspaper version was copied on the typewriter; and the now world-famous author began a reconsideration of his first long work.

The opening pages of the typescript, discovered among Gorky's papers after his death, reveal considerable changes in the author's own handwriting. Further on, the notes are restricted mainly to minor corrections of style. All of Gorky's notes are incorporated in the present translation.

Besides its intrinsic worth as a piece of writing, this first novel by Gorky has special significance to the reader who is interested in tracing from its origins the artistic development of one of the greatest and most spectacular figures in Russian literature. With this reader in mind, we are including with the novel Gorky's heretofore untranslated essay "How I Became a Writer". Written towards the end of his life, this retrospective essay might very well have been used by Gorky himself as the open sesame to his collected works.

A. M. Krich
THE PURSUIT PRESS

ORPHAN PAUL

1

The parents of my hero were very modest people. Wishing to maintain anonymity, they abandoned their infant son near a fence on one of the deserted streets of the town and disappeared into the dark night. Apparently there was in their hearts little pride in their own creation; nor did they have the moral strength necessary to make of their son a person bearing no resemblance to his parents.

If they were really guided by this last consideration the night they decided to give their child into

LIBRARY
SOUTHERN SEMINARY

11

the trust of society, it was indicated by the terse note pinned to the rags in which the infant was wrapped: "Christened. Paul." They could not have been altogether stupid, for the vast majority of fathers and mothers are motivated by the desire to give their children those very habits, prejudices, ideas and attitudes on which they themselves have wasted so much of their lives.

For some time, after he was shoved against the fence, little Paul took it like a true fatalist. He lay quiet, blandly sucking the piece of bread wrapped in cheesecloth which had been put into his mouth. When he was bored with this, he pushed it out with his tongue and emitted a small sound which scarcely disturbed the stillness of the night.

It was an August night, dark and fresh. One felt the approach of Fall. Pliant birch branches on which there were already many yellowing leaves, some of which had fallen to the ground, curved over little Paul. From time to time, the leaves silently detached themselves from the branches, hesitatingly twirled in the moist, dense air and slowly fell to the ground. It had rained during the day. Toward evening the sun, in setting, had managed to heat the ground thoroughly.

Sometimes the leaves fell on Paul's little red face, scarcely visible in the thick bundle of rags so pains-

12

takingly and tightly wrapped by a mother's hand. When this happened Paul would grimace and blink. He endured this until he succeeded in unwrapping the rags and exposing his tiny body to the dampness of the night. Then, feeling free, he lifted his little foot to his mouth, and began to suck it, silently, but with apparent pleasure.

But you must pardon me. Here I am speaking *a priori* of the behaviour of the child during his sojourn by the fence. I was not a witness to it myself. Only the beautiful, deep sky, generously studded with golden stars, saw him. And the heavens, in spite of the fact that they are so much on the lips of poets, and in the prayers of true believers, were indifferent, as always, to the affairs of Earth.

If I had seen Paul there by the fence, I, of course, would have been filled with passionate indignation against his parents and deep compassion for the child personally. I would have called the police immediately. Then I would have gone home feeling proud of myself. Anyone in my place would have done the same. I really believe this. But no one was there, and so the inhabitants of the town were deprived of an easy way of demonstrating their better feelings. Most people find the display of their better side an engaging and absorbing occupation — provided it does not interfere with other, competing interests.

But no one was there. Finally Paul became thoroughly chilled. His foot came out of his mouth. Quiet whimpers, then loud cries, disturbed the stillness of the night.

He did not have to cry long, for in half an hour a man, wrapped in something that made him resemble a large moving tree-stump, walked up and bent over him. Thickly murmuring, "bastards," he spat explosively to one side. Then he lifted the child and wrapped him in the rags as carefully as he could. He crammed the baby into his coat, thus, at one and the same time, shutting out the piercing air and Paul's crying.

"Good God, another one tossed aside! The bastards! That makes three this summer. Curses! Another! Sinning, sinning . . . more sinning! I spit on them!"

This was Klim Vislov, night watchman, a man of strict morals, whose morality, however, did not interfere with his being an inveterate drunkard and a fervent devotee of the three levels of profanity—mother, father and soul.

"Cart him over to the station house!"
This command was given by petty constable Kar-

penko, the foremost Don Juan of the third section of town. He had a reddish pointed moustache and a bold eye with which he was quickly able to inflame the heart of any girl. The command was directed to Arefi Gibly, a policeman, a gloomy, round-shouldered man, a lover of solitude, books, and singing birds, and a terrible hater of chatter, cab-drivers and women.

Arefi Gibly took little Paul in his arms and was about to go off, but suddenly stopped and unwrapped the rags covering the baby's face. He looked at the child for a few seconds, then touched his cheek, bent over him, screwed up his mouth and clicked his tongue.

Paul was again quietly sucking on his piece of bread, not at all interested in making out precisely what Arefi Gibly wished to express with his strange gestures. He replied only with a lifted brow, which of course did not express anything definite, clear or understandable.

Then Arefi Gibly smiled so broadly that his moustaches jumped up toward his nose. His tremendous deep black beard shook and moved toward his ears. As he walked along the street, he questioned little Paul in a loud voice, "A future human being, ha?" — to which the child nodded affirmatively and gurgled.

"Chaha! Oo-fee! Kru-kru-kru! Gur-bur!" Arefi Gibly cooed like an elephant. He sat on the curbstone near a lamp post, intent on the face of the child, as if awaiting some reaction.

The baby was perplexed, not understanding Arefi's jargon. He shook his head several times, lifted his eyebrows indifferently, but did not permit the bread to slip out of his mouth.

Arefi burst into peals of laughter.

"Don't like it, hunh? Oh you—mosquito!"

At this, "the mosquito," evidently convinced he was being offered nothing, opened his mouth and eyes wide. He looked puzzled, but was really choking on the bread.

Arefi hurriedly jerked it out, and then peered into the face of the child in anxious concentration, as if wishing to convince himself that he had not torn the mouth clear off.

Paul coughed.

"Shoo. Shoo." Arefi Gibly hissed like a locomotive, letting out steam. He swung the child through the air, convinced that his manouvre would stop the cough. But the baby coughed still louder.

"Oh, you!" sighed Arefi, bewildered, looking around helplessly.

The street was asleep. Infrequent lights flickered along both sides. Off in the distance, the lights seemed to be more compact, closer together. But the whole street was dim; it seemed to be leaning on some sort of black wall which reached almost to the sky spread over it. The lively, flickering rays of its bright stars shone like a smile.

Arefi glanced down—away from the black wall.

There was the town, a mass of dark buildings, one shoved close to the other, lit by the dim, recurring lights of the lamps. Infrequent, scarcely audible noises were born and died, lazily, indifferently.

The sight nauseated Arefi. He pressed Paul tightly to the coarse cloth of his jacket. He pressed him close to his breast and sighed deeply, looking up into the distant heaven. Paul was now through coughing and ready to yell.

"Filth!"

Having made so eloquent a resume of his own feeling about the town, Arefi rose from the curbstone and walked up the street. He bounced the baby in his arms, as evenly and carefully as he could. He turned from one street into another for some time. Apparently he was burdened with some special, unusual thoughts, for he failed to notice, along the entire road, how the streets narrowed here, widened there, one crossing the other, met—and suddenly he was in the town square. But he noticed the square only when he found himself in front of a fountain with two lamp posts on either side. This fountain stood in the center of the square. Arefi had already gone past the police station.

Cursing, he turned back. The lamplight fell over Arefi's shoulder on the small face of Paul, tightly pressed to the gray cloth coat.

"Asleep!" Arefi whispered, not taking his eyes off the child. He felt an uncomfortable tickling of the throat. To rid himself of this sensation, he quietly blew his nose. He thought, perhaps it would be better if children were able to foresee the irrational complications of life from the very first days of their lives. If this were so, the future man in his arms would not sleep so soundly. He probably would have yelled for all he was worth.

Arefi Gibly was a policeman and a middle-aged man, so he knew life. And he knew that if you don't assert yourself at least by a single shout, even a policeman won't notice you. And if you cannot attract attention, you perish, for man does not last long alone. This thoughtless baby would surely perish, for, at this crucial moment, he was asleep.

"Hello, there!" Arefi shouted reproachfully, walking under the arch into the station house.

"Where'd you come from?" asked a gray-coated co-worker, appearing unexpectedly before him.

"Off my beat."

18

The other yawned blissfully as he poked a finger into Paul's cheek.

"What's that?"

"Quiet, you fool! It's a baby."

"The devil with you! What are you blathering about?"

"Who's on duty?"

"Gogolev."

"Sleeping?"

"Dead to the world!"

"How about Marya?"

"She's sleeping too. Why shouldn't she be?"

"Uh-huh. That's true . . ." Arefi Gibly drawled. He was thoughtful, did not move.

"Soon I'll be off duty. Then I can go to sleep, too!" the other remarked and started to leave.

"Wait a minute, Mikhailo!" Arefi pulled at his sleeve with his free hand. Then he whispered confidentially:

"How about talking to Marya now? What do you think?"

"That's all she needs!" Mikhailo laughed ironically, glancing into Paul's peaceful sleeping face. "Brother, she's fed up with her own kids."

"Why it's only for one night!" Arefi said in a tone he thought convincing.

"What's that to me? It's only—you know her,—

19

she'll kick me out . . . Well, give him here and I'll see."

Arefi carefully transferred little Paul from his own arms to Mikhailo's. He followed, on tip-toe, down the corridor, peering intently over the shoulder of his friend at the face of the sleeping tot. He held his breath as Mikhailo's heavy boots thumped loudly on the stone floor of the corridor. They reached the door.

"I'll wait here," Arefi whispered.

Mikhailo opened the door and disappeared.

Arefi stood still. He felt disturbed, depressed. He tore a thread from the cuff of his coat. He stroked his beard energetically. He picked bits of plaster from the wall. None of this made him feel any better.

Behind the door there was the sound of muted quarrelling.

"She swore, but she took him!" Mikhailo announced, opening the door. There was a triumphant, victorious expression on his clean-shaven face.

"Well, that's that!" Arefi Gibly sighed in relief. They both walked toward the exit.

"Good-by, brother. I'm going back to my post."

"O.K. Get going!" Mikhailo answered indifferently. He went into a corner and rustled up some straw, apparently preparing a bunk for himself.

Arefi started down the stairway slowly. When he

reached the third step, he felt that his feet were somehow stuck to the flagstones. He stood still for several minutes. Finally, the following dialogue took place in the dim lamplit corridor:

"Mike?"

"Now what?"

"You'll give him away to-morrow?"

"Hunh? The kid? Well, of course!"

"To the foundling home?"

"No, you fool, to the blacksmith!"

A pause. Mikhailo rustled the straw in his corner bunk. His boots shuffled along the floor. Arefi looked out over the sleeping town. The black night merged the houses into one gray, solid wall. The dark lines of the streets seemed like deep gaps. There, at the end of town, off to the left, was the foundling home. It was a large, stone building, coldly white, severe in appearance, with large indifferent, empty windows. No flowers, no curtains. . . .

"He'll die there!" grumbled Arefi.

"The kid? Probably. It's very seldom they don't die there. Because—you know—the cleanliness, the order. . . ."

But here Mikhailo, overcome with sleep, began to snore. His opinion of the destructive effect of cleanliness and order on the young was left without further emphasis or elaboration.

Arefi stood a while longer; then went back to his beat.

He arrived there when the night had already paled and the air had become fresh at the approach of morning. His hut was located almost in the fields. Now, it appeared to him to be more solitary, more detached from the rest of the town than it had ever seemed before. Previously, this had not given rise to any special thought or feeling, but to-day, it did. He sat in front of the door, on the bench flanked by mis-shapen elder bushes. Arefi's gray, humped figure seemed to fuse with their dark background.

He pondered. His thinking was weighty, slow. A great deal of time was necessary for his thought to become finally crystallized into the form of a single question: Do people have a right to give birth to children if they can't rear them?

After having almost dislocated his brain, Arefi Gibly finally answered this question with a firm and conclusive "No, they haven't!" Then he felt better. He sighed deeply, and shaking his fist threateningly into space, muttered through his teeth: "The dirty bastards!"

The sun rose. Its first rays struck the windows of the hut, turning fiery gold on the glass. The two windows seemed to be the huge, laughing eyes of a strange monster with a sharp, green head, rising from

22

the ground to look on God's earth. The elder bushes, crawling upon the roof, almost seemed like that monster's mop of hair. The cracks over the door were the furrows on his happy, smiling forehead.

2

The next day at noon Arefi sat in Marya's house. She had sharp features, green eyes. In a dirty dress, her skirt tucked up high and her sleeves rolled up, her every movement was a poem of aggressive energy.

Arefi Gibly had a great deal to say to her, but he was not in the habit of talking and so felt very awkward with her. Marya's calm, deliberate movements oppressed him with their self-assurance and strength. He was a woman-hater and he could not conceal it; it was evident in his sullen glances at Marya's broad face, in his explosive spitting on the floor.

Little Paul lay in a heap of rags on a bunk propped up by reed chairs. He was engrossed in a gymnastic exercise—catching his foot in his hands and then trying to put it in his mouth. The red chubby foot did not obey, and little Paul, apparently not displeased, emitted approving sounds.

"Well, you atheist! What are you going to do with him now?" Marya began, sitting down opposite Arefi and wiping her face with her apron. "I won't take him. I can't. Turn him over to old Kitaeva. She'll raise him for you for two rubles. The infant's already more than a month old. He's a healthy, quiet baby. He'll be no trouble. Give him to her."

"And what if she starves him to death?"

"Starve him to death? Why should she starve him?" Marya teased.

"Why? . . . she's a woman, well, and . . ."

"You tongue-tied mummy! I'll just take him to her and that's that! He'll just be son No. 71 to her. Ha, ha, ha! . . . Dope! Starve him! And who do you think raises babies, — devils like you? Woman! A woman is all strength! And who raises devils like you? Do you think you're hammered out on a blacksmith's anvil? You've got some right to talk!"

"Don't you go barking at me," Arefi remarked,

trying to get to the point and avoiding Marya's eye which seemed to be fixed on him in a special sort of a way. "I didn't mean that. I was thinking of . . ."

"Shut up — that's enough! I won't change my ways just to please you, you know! Look who's talking! What an important personage! Is it possible that my language is so strong that you'd die of it? Do you think I can talk to you in any other way? A man like you should be beaten regularly every hour."

"All right, all right. Talk sense."

Arefi felt the urge to curse the aggressive woman roundly. He tried to suppress the feeling and, finding it almost impossible, became more and more ill at ease.

"Come on, tell me what to do and I'll go. I can't stand your talk."

"Ah, how tender we are! You blockhead!"

This speech evidently sapped all of Marya's bellicose aggressiveness and exhausted her lexicon of uncomplimentary epithets. She did not cease for a moment to bustle about the littered room, doing everything at the same time; cooking, sewing, one minute feeding this infant, then that one, distributing them on the stove, behind the stove, behind the curtain screening the bed, shouting through the window to the hens and again turning back to the babies who poked their heads into every corner and gave full play to their vocal powers. Finally, she straightened up before Arefi, her hands akimbo, and lectured him thus:

"First of all, you go to the sergeant and say 'I'm taking the child myself.' Then bring me two rubles for a month in advance. I'll give it to old Kitaeva. And another ruble for a little shirt, a little blanket. . . . Well, and other things. And then—get out of here! I'm fed up with you—you dummy!"

Arefi rose, sighed deeply and went out in silence.

In the evening old Kitaeva came to see Marya. She had a blind left eye and a face that looked like a withered radish both in color and shape. Her chin was adorned with a small gray imperial beard. She spoke in a squeaky, thin voice, bothering one or another of the saints with every second or third word, calling upon them, directly or indirectly, either to vouch for the veracity of her words, or for no reason at all.

Marya dryly explained the situation to her, gave her instructions, and concluded with this admonition:

"Now you be careful! You can go so far and no farther. Know your limit!" She shook her finger threateningly at Kitaeva.

Old Kitaeva compressed herself into a small ball,

bowed low to Marya. Wallowing in a feeling of self-abasement, she simpered slavishly, almost in a whisper:

"Marya Timofeyevna, my dear! You know me! To somebody else maybe, but not to you . . ." and here she nodded her head, as if to indicate that she could say much more, but had not the strength.

"That's just it. I know you, you pious old fraud! Oh, yes!"

This was said with exaggerated emphasis, far from complimentary to the old woman.

All this time little Paul lay quietly on the bunk. Only when old Kitaeva took him into her arms, whispering reverently "Lord have mercy upon us!" did he emit a disapproving whimper. Then he became quiet again, completely indifferent to his fate, and remained so until he was taken out into the street. There, he grimaced to cut off the sun shining into his eyes, but this did not help much. Then he shook his head with no better effect. The sun beat down on his face and burned through the thin skin of his cheeks. He began to howl.

"You little rascal! Back there in the house you were still, quietly pretending, but no sooner do I take you out than you begin to whine. Well, now, you lie still!"

Old Kitaeva tossed him from one arm to the other

and walked on. Recently, old Kitaeva's schedule had been determined by five little throats eternally raving with hunger, not giving her a moment of quiet and rest . . . Oh, heavens! I've taken on another one; now I'll have six, she thought. They're a bother, sure enough, but the good thing is that, although you don't get enough to eat, you don't die of hunger either.

The diagonal rays of the sun dodged into the apartment through the dim, old, green window, its cracks sealed with putty which made a pattern in the glass. And it seemed as if the sun-rays withered and shrank from the thick smell of ammonia which filled the two low rooms. The ceilings were smoky, the wall-paper torn and dirty, and the floors, ornamented with large cracks, were squeaky.

The first room, known as the children's room, was laid out in Spartan simplicity: three long, wide benches laden with trash, and that was all. The room was so dirty that apparently even the flies could not find enough strength to live in the midst of such filth, for, having circled a little while in the smelly atmosphere of the children's room, they were soon overcome, and, in protest, buzzed quickly into the other room, or into the hall through an open door quilted with something faintly resembling dark green oil-cloth.

The second room was separated from the children's by a partition with a small crooked door cut in it. Directly opposite the door was a table on which stood a discolored samovar bent over to one side. The samovar was an invalid, wounded in several places, always whistling and grumbling in a hypochondriacal fashion. It was exactly in keeping with the general squalor of old Kitaeva's household.

There seemed to be no one in either of the rooms. With the exception of the disappointed buzzing of the flies and the grumbling noises of the samovar, no sound could be heard. But the impression of complete desertion disappeared when one looked into the dark corner near the door. There, on the bench, something alive stirred. Lifted in mid-air and twisted into an arch was a leg. An attentive listener could just make out a scarcely audible monotonous whimpering.

The owner of this leg, and of still another one just as twisted, green, and withered with rickets, was a baby, a year and a half old. Old Kitaeva called him Horse-Radish when she was annoyed with him. She supplied all her charges with such more or less witty and apt nicknames. Horse-Radish suited the rickety baby perfectly. Wrinkled as if with old age, withered, distorted by sickness, an unchanging expression of bitter perplexity seemed to have been frozen on his small wizened face. It was as though he were trying to find out who was responsible for bringing him into this world such an outlandish cripple; to guess who had played such a cruel, callous joke on him, and why. Though he seemed to be making an effort to find out, he also seemed to be convinced of the futility of such an attempt, and thus he was eternally broken in spirit.

For days on end he lay there in the corner. Lifting now this, now that one of his twisted legs, he looked at them long and fixedly. His deep eyes had the staring concentration and sadly serious expression which so often gleam in the eyes of sick children. He would examine his legs and mumble very, very softly. His pale, bloodless lips exposed his toothless gums and a little yellow-coated tongue. His arms, which he could not move, were cramped into a ring, their wrists propped up against his armpits. Though his legs from the knees up were in good condition, from the knees downward they bent in an arc, crossing at the ankles. Sometimes he seemed bored by the study of his legs. Then, with the same immutable expression of perplexity, he would raise his eyes to the ceiling where he could see a quivering sun-spot made by the rays of the sun coming through the window, reflected in a tub of water and then on to the ceiling. But, apparently suspecting that an intimate acquaintance with the rays of the sun would avail him nothing, he would transfer his serious eyes from the ceiling again toward his feet which seemed to interest him more than anything else. He found little of interest in the rays of the sun for he felt that soon everything worldly would disappear, his ability to see and think; he himself, in the near future, would be transferred from above to below ground.

He had been living with old Kitaeva for eighteen months, but she had been paid for only two months. Now she waited with great impatience for the time when he would "vacate her apartment," as she euphemistically expressed it.

Once she had gone to the apartment of his mother, a small, anaemic, stooped seamstress, and found her lying on a cot, barely alive.

"Well, my dear," said old Kitaeva, sitting down on the cot where the mother lay, scarcely moving. "You've had strength enough to give birth, but you don't have any left to feed him. That's bad! But, I'm not obliged to bear the burden of your sins. Hand over some money or take your child back. I'm no Lady Bountiful."

The mother's dull blue eyes opened wide, expressing deep sorrow and terror.

"Granny!" she began in a choking whisper. "I'll pay! I'll pay up to the last kopek, to the last kopek! I'll pay. I'll rip the skin off my live body and sell it, and pay you! I'll become a prostitute! . . . Have patience, please! Take pity on me, on me and on him, the poor boy . . . Ai, ai, ai . . . have pity!"

Old Kitaeva listened to her groans and saw the big tears roll down her sunken, withered cheeks. She saw the sunken chest heave.

"You wenches! Shameless wenches! You should be beaten good and hard! Oh, yes!" she reprimanded.

"Oh, Granny! He loved me, he wanted to marry me! . . ."

"That, my dear, is an old song. I've heard it a thousand times."

But it seemed that old Kitaeva had not only heard the song, but had sung it herself. She made a face, coughed, bent over, thought a while, and, kissing the sick woman, went away, firmly ordering her to get well. But the latter disobeyed the order and died. Horse-Radish remained in old Kitaeva's trust. She was soon fed up with him. Then she placed him in a corner and hoped that Nature would take its course. She consoled herself with the thought that he could not last long anyway, thus quieting her conscience as much as she could.

There were four others in addition to Horse-

Radish. Three were paid for on time; the fourth went out begging and what he brought more than paid for his own keep. He was a chubby, round, rosy-cheeked six year old brat, Gurka Ball, a daredevil of a boy and a great favorite with old Kitaeva.

"You'll become a first-class crook, Gurka!" she would praise him in the evenings upon his return from begging. At these times he would pull out from his knapsack chunks of bread, tops of samovars, door knobs, weights, toys, candlesticks, small frying pans, and similar junk.

"Oh, what a crook I'll be! I'll steal everything— even horses!"

"And what if the cops send you off to Siberia, eh?" old Kitaeva asked with caressing kindness.

"I'll run away!" Gurka answered readily.

Then old Kitaeva would give him seven kopeks and send him out to play.

The other three children did not differ one from the other. They had not yet managed to acquire any definite individual traits. All three yelled very loudly if they were not fed for a long time. They also yelled when they were overfed, when old Kitaeva would forget to give them a drink, and when they were forcibly made to drink. They also cried for a good many other reasons, but these reasons, individually or collectively, never seemed important to the old woman, for she screamed at the children with such energetic intensity that the chorus of noises of all the babies was drowned out. Generally speaking, they were restless infants, every day demanding food, drink, dry diapers, air, and other things for which they could hardly have had the right, for they had not yet lived; they had only begun to live. Because old Kitaeva had such a utilitarian point of view, she did not pamper them, apparently wishing them to become self-reliant, capable of acquiring by themselves everything necessary for their well-being.

Old Kitaeva's day would begin in this way:

Gurka Ball was the first of the five to get up in the morning. He slept in old Kitaeva's room, separated from his four co-boarders. Upon opening his eyes, he would immediately leap out of his bed, made of boxes, fumble under his pillow and drag out a long rooster feather. He would tip-toe carefully into the children's room, trying to avoid a squeak, open the door, and just as carefully walk across the floor. In the summer, the dried-up floor boards would make creaky noises; in the winter, one plank would thump dully against the other. And so Gurka would steal up to one of the infants still asleep. He would lean over and begin to tickle his nose with the feather. The baby would twist his head from one side to the other, frown in a ridiculous fashion, and rub his nose with his fist. Hardly able to restrain his laughter, Gurka would puff up like a red balloon and continue. Finally, the infant would wake and yell. Soon a second, then a third, would sympathetically imitate the first, while Gurka would yell "granny" with all his might, run from one infant to the other, hiss like a snake, make faces, blow into their nostrils, and generally amuse himself to his heart's content.

A concert would ensue, outlandish in volume and cacophony. The children coughed, sneezed, howled, choked, cried—as if they were being fried in a pan.

Horse-Radish was never bothered. Gurka was afraid of his staring, pensive eyes, constantly examining his legs. Once, coming up to Horse-Radish with the intention of including him among his victims, Gurka saw those eyes fixed upon him. They looked like the eyes, not of a child, but of a cop. Gurka, for a number of reasons, could not be at ease with a policeman. He would respectfully step aside upon meeting one. Gurka backed away from Horse-Radish and never again bothered the rickety child.

"Oh — ho — ho! They've begun to howl! . . . They've begun to beg! . . . To screech! . . . Let them!" Old Kitaeva, waking up, would recall several uncensored epithets, repeating them many times in all their variations.

Gurka, assuming a serious mien, would go into

37

the other room, puff up like a balloon, and then drag the samovar into tlie hall where he would rattle it unnecessarily. In general, this happy youngster liked to produce noise, and the more stupendous the noise, the happier he was.

Old Kitaeva gently pulled the wet diapers from under the babies.

"Go on, bawl, little devils! Yawn! Little frogs!"

At home old Kitaeva would not call on the holy fathers and martyrs, felling that she herself was a martyr.

The infants whimpered, Gurka thundered and thumped, old Kitaeva swore. The noise would wake the neighbors who would have come to the unmistakable conclusion that it was already six in the morning.

The noise and yelling would continue for two hours until the old woman managed to change the diapers, wash and feed the babies. Then she would sit down to tea. By this time, Gurka would have finished his. He would seize his knapsack, convert it into a cap, put it on his head, and run off to beg.

After tea, the old woman would drag the children out into the yard where she would seat them on boxes filled with fine, dry sand. The babies would bake in the sun for about three hours until dinner time. During this time old Kitaeva would wash diapers, sew, mend, swear, feed the children and be "torn into a thousand pieces," as she used to say.

Sometimes two or three friends would drop by. They were women of various sizes and of two professions; one of which landed you in jail, the other, sooner or later, brought you to a hospital.

Two or three bottles would always accompany these friends. In a short time the air in the street and the ears of the neighbors would be assailed by a bitter song about "double-crossers and rogues", or other such ditties. Somewhat later, select expletives would be heard, then a cry of "help!", and finally, one of two things would happen; either the friends would drag old Kitaeva along the ground by her hair, or old Kitaeva and one of her friends would hit the others. But the result was always the same; first a deep sleep, then a friendly reconciliation.

During such times, the babies would be left alone. They would shout at the top of their lungs and could easily have died of hunger or succumbed to rupture from their yelling had not someone come to their rescue. For, about the time when the fighting-mad, belligerent friends would be overcome with exhaustion, in a dark corner of the yard, a small door would open in a shanty that rose from the ground. An obese, pock-marked woman would come out.

She would emerge, yawn, cover her mouth with

her hand, and look at the sky with glazed, expressionless eyes. Walking up to one of the sand boxes she would pull out an infant and sit squarely down in the same box. Then, slowly unbuttoning the collar of her dress, she would shove the child's head into her bosom. A hungry sucking sound would ensue.

Nothing was reflected on the face of the obese woman which would have permitted the observer to conclude that her efforts were prompted by kindness. Her face was quite pock-marked and very dull. That was all there was to see.

Having fed one, she would go to another, to a third, and finally she would walk into the room where Horse-Radish lay. First, she would take him in her arms and carry him over the window. The baby would blink and turn his head away from the light falling upon him. Then the obese woman would walk out of the room into the yard and, sitting on one of the sand boxes, would offer the infant her breast. He would suck lazily while she stroked his pallid head and cheeks. When he had finished she would place him in the box and heap the sand over his broken, rickety little body until only his head was visible.

Apparently this gave Horse-Radish a great deal of pleasure for his eyes would shine and the fixed expression on his face would disappear. Then the obese woman would smile. Far from adding charm to her face, this made it appear even wider than usual. She fussed with the infant for a long time, until his grumbling made her realize that he had been burned by the sand and sun. Then she would take him up in her arms and silently rock him. He seemed pleased, for he would smile in his sleep. She would kiss him and carry him into the room. Then she would walk out into the courtyard and look at the infants in the sand, the same wooden expression on her face. Sometimes, if they were not sleep, she would play with them, feed them again, and disappear behind the small door of the shanty off in the corner of the yard. From there, she would look out through the partly open door. If, when night fell, Kitaeva still lay in her trance, the obese woman would again emerge and put the children to bed.

Do not think that I am here portraying some kind fairy. Oh, no! She was nothing but a pock-marked woman with tremendous, baggy breasts. And she was mute. She was simply the wife of a drunken smith. Once her husband had struck her on the head so clumsily that she bit her tongue in half. At first he was very much grieved by this. Then he began to call her a dumb monster. And that was all.

This is how the boarders lived in the home of old

Kitaeva in the summer time. In the winter they lived somewhat differently—the sand boxes were on the stove instead of in the court yard. Old Kitaeva considered sand an important factor in the physical development of infants.

The upbringing of little Paul did not differ in any respect from that of his co-boarders, except that sometimes a big, black beard would bend over his box of sand; black, deep eyes would look at him long and attentively.

At first Paul was frightened by this apparition, but gradually he became accustomed to it. So much so that he began to poke his small hands into the straggling beard which tickled him. Nor was he any longer afraid of the dull, mumbling sounds that came through the large glistening teeth visible in the middle of the beard. Sometimes he was taken out of the sand by two powerful arms which threw his little body high in the air. Little Paul screwed up his face and was quiet from fear. When the rocking stopped he would shriek lustily. Then the tremendous black man standing before him would cry out:

"Hey, woman! Don't you hear?"

"I hear, man, I hear!" Kitaeva would answer in irritation and crawl out from somewhere. "Sh, sh, it's nothing, little one, it's nothing! Ooh, ooh, ah, ah . . ."

"Why are they yelling so?" the bass voice thundered in the court yard.

"Yelling, old man, yelling. All of them yell, as many as there are!" the quivering falsetto would ring back ironically.

"You don't keep them clean—they're dirty."

"Yes, dirty, man, dirty. Very dirty."

The bass mumbled in perplexity and the falsetto coughed.

"Couldn't things be done better?" retorted the bass.

"It's possible, possible. It could be better, very much better, it could be!" the falsetto jeered.

"Then why not do something about it?" the bass threatened.

"Oh, well, my dear. I'm just an old woman, helpless, poor, that's what's the matter. That's what it is. There it is," the falsetto said submissively.

A pause.

"Sh . . . sh . . . sh . . . Sleep. Slee--ee--eep! Slee--ee--ee--pp," whistled through the air.

"Well, good-by. Take care!" the bass dropped an octave.

"I'll take care, man, I'll take care," the falsetto answered softly.

Then there was the noise of heavy, retreating steps.

3

Four years later the child Paul came to live in Arefi Gibly's hut. He was a short-legged, large-headed creature with dark eyes set deep in a face marred by smallpox.

Paul was not a talkative child and always seemed to be looking at something visible only to himself. And so his coming did not seem to disturb the lonely routine existence of the occupant of the policeman's hut. During these four years, Arefi Gibly's head and beard had developed silvery gray strands. He had become more solemn and had acquired an even greater love for books dealing with the lives of the holy saints.

Paul's days flowed on evenly and quietly. Early in the morning he would be wakened by the birds who would begin their loud conversations with the first rays of the sun. Paul would open his eyes and from his bed behind the stove, look at them for a long time as they hopped in their cages from perch to perch, splashed in the water, nibbled at the seeds, and sang, each in his own fashion. They sang enthusiastically, energetically and far from beautifully. The happy strumming of the greenfinches, the monotonous whistling of the goldfinches, and the ridiculous squeaking of the bullfinches would fuse into a strange rippling flow of sound that filled the small, smoky, crowded room.

There was also a taciturn, crippled starling. He was alone in a large wire cage hanging over the window. He would cling to the perch with one foot, rolling his body from side to side, constantly turning his head. Suddenly, he would let out a long thin whistle, throwing the other birds into a state of puzzled silence, for they would break off their discordant symphony and look about as if trying to understand the import of this strange whistle. Then the starling's neighbor, the bullfinch, substantial as a general, with red feathers on his breast, would fly into a rage and puff himself up. He would fidget about, poke his head in the direction of the starling, rattle and hiss in a most unbirdlike fashion, open his beak and stick out his thick tongue. But the starling, swaying from side to side, would pay no attention and turn his head about philosophically. His still black figure became lively only when a cockroach crawled into the cage; but even this animation would last but two or three seconds. There was something deep and skeptical in the whole conduct of the starling, particularly in his whistle, that had a sobering effect on the other birds. It sounded as if the weighty word of a wise, aged man were uttered amid the fiery, optimistic speeches of youth. Sometimes the starling would suddenly begin to jump in the cage, fluttering his wings. He would open his beak, pluck his feathers, and assume an important, firm attitude as if about to whistle— but he would not whistle. He would fall again into his philosophic silence as if to indicate that the time had not yet come for his act, or as if he were convinced that nothing he could ever do would change the existing order of things.

Paul liked the starling better than the other birds because he saw in him a resemblance to Uncle Arefi. Uncle Arefi also liked the starling; his cage was the first to be cleaned and supplied with fresh seeds and water.

In the morning Paul would lie in bed until Arefi came. For some reason Uncle Arefi did not seem to like his hut. Most of the time, day and night, he would be out of it. Uncle Arefi would open the door very slowly and very carefully, poke his dark head into the room, and ask:

"Are you up?"

"M'up!" Paul would answer.

Then Uncle Arefi would go out to start the samovar. The samovar was very old, with numerous patches of coarse, dull pieces of tin. In place of one handle, there was a piece of horse-shoe, fastened to the side with wire. Having started the samovar, Arefi would clean the cages and sweep the floor until he heard the thin whistle of the samovar. Then, apparently wishing to make his voice appear gentler, he would shout to Paul in an unusually thick bass voice:

"Get up and wash. Say your prayers!"

Paul would get up, wash, and say his prayers. He would do these things calmly, quietly, with a serious, set mouth, very much in the manner of a grown-up who is deeply convinced of the necessity and importance of the work he is doing. This mien, together with his dishevelled hair and serious glistening eyes, made him resemble a young mole intent upon the work of the coming day. Then, washed and combed, under Arefi's tutelage, he would read the morning prayer in an artificially subdued voice, then seat himself at the table in front of the funny, misshapen samovar. By this time, he would already have lost much of his wild charm, his air of stiff importance would have become somewhat funny.

They drank tea in silence, and in the same silence, they would spend the larger part of the day. After tea, Arefi would cook. That is, in the winter he would heat the stove, pour water into the pot, throw vegetables into it, and then a piece of meat. He would put the pot into the fire with his bare hands. In the summer, he would make a tiny bonfire in the small court yard behind the hut and bake potatoes over it. So that he might not subject himself to the indignity of having to borrow methods from women, he would cook simple things. Braving danger to his health, he would not allow himself to use forks, rolling-pins, churns, and other noble attributes of the work of women, although he owned such utensils.

Paul, dressed in checkered little pants and a bright red shirt, followed Arefi around with an air of importance, intently watching everything he did. He would rarely put questions to Uncle Arefi. Arefi's one-syllabled, sullen answers did not inspire Paul with a desire to continue conversation. For a while he would watch Arefi as he fussed about in the hut. Then he would go out into the street, followed by the injunction not to go far.

The hut stood at the edge of town. Its windows faced a field through which ran a steel gray strip of river. Beyond, there was another field, green and inviting in summer, cold and lonely in winter. Still farther on, the walls of the forest supported the horizon. In the daytime it was still, dark, and silent. In the evening, when the sun set behind it, it was decorated with purple and gold rays.

Paul would go off to the river, sit on the rocks among the willows, and throw chips into the water in order to watch them as they floated off into the distance. The rays of the sun played on the water, the wind covered it with a dancing ripple. Often, lulled by the busy rustling of the waves against the shore, he would fall asleep.

If Arefi was at home at the time, he would come and get Paul. They would have dinner; then Paul would again go off to the river until evening. He played there alone or with Tulka, the pauper, a cross-eyed, thieving girl of eight. She was dirty, noisy. Arefi disliked her. When she came to the hut, he chased her out.

Toward evening Paul would look at the setting sun and see the live, beautiful forest die, be engulfed in the evening shadows. Then he would return to the house and go to sleep. When Arefi was in, he would first say his prayers. But when Arefi was out, there were no prayers, no undressing.

And so the days ran one after another, monotonous, quiet, and, as always happens with days, they made a chain, creating weeks, months, years. . . . Paul grew; his days became complicated. He began to wonder whither the river flows; what is hidden behind the forest; why the big clouds float freely through the skies; why a small stone, thrown upward, falls to the ground. He wondered what was going on in town where the roofs were crowded so closely together, and what was happening beyond the town, and, generally, in the world which was so noisy in the daytime and so quiet at night. But he did not turn to Arefi with these questions. Perhaps he thought that a man who was so quiet knows nothing. Arefi's silence and his sullen face perplexed the boy.

When Mikhailo came on one of his infrequent visits, Paul, sitting in a corner, would get his fill of human conversation. Mikhailo talked a great deal, and always began by asking Arefi:

"Well, monk? Still alive? Not thinking of getting married?" and then he would guffaw as Arefi sat wrapped in cold indifference.

But this indifference did not faze Mikhailo in the least. He would wipe his clean-shaven face with a handkerchief and, seating himself comfortably on a bench, "would harp on the same old thing", as his sullen friend termed it when he was irritated.

"To-day, brother, I ate pretty damn well. Marya cooked a German wheat kasha for me. Oh, what a kasha! . . . with milk and raisins, too. Eh? It was good! When it comes to cooking, Marya has golden hands. And when it comes to a good many other things, too. Sewing, and that sort of thing, she can do everything! Ah, a good woman, my wife! You should have such a woman, Arefi, hunh? Such a woman, hunh?"

"She barks like a dog!" Arefi would retort tersely, fussing about the samovar or already sitting at the table and dipping his mustaches in a saucer of tea.

Mikhailo would lift his brows in surprise.

"Bark, you say? So what? Well, supposing she does? That's true! You know damn well that a man and his wife can't get along without it. Can't be done! Everybody wants to feel that he's boss and nobody wants to give in. Take me, for instance. Would I give in? Not on your life! For instance, if I yell, 'Marya!', and if she doesn't listen to reason

". . . she gets a smack in the teeth, that's what!"

"And she gives you two," Arefi Gibly answered coldly.

"Two? Well, suppose she does! . . . What about two? Isn't she my wife? She has the right to smack me twice. But I wouldn't give in even then. I'd give her such a sound thrashing . . ."

"And she'd keel you over with a rolling pin, like the last time . . ." Arefi said, not conceding.

"A ro-o-l-l-ing pin! . . . Damn you! Do you think she thrashes me with a rolling pin every day? Sure, it happened. Once. That's all. A rolling pin! Why bring that up?"

Silence. The friends drank their tea and looked at each other.

"Well, and how are your birds? Alive?"

"Look for yourself."

"I see. Good. Birds — that's wonderful. I think I'll get some birds too."

"Your wife would roast them," Arefi said ironically.

"Never! She likes birds herself. Why, recently she even bought a goose. And how she bought it!" Mikhailo suddenly livened up. "Smart! She's a sly one! She sees a drunken peasant and immediately begins to shout at him. You, she says, you're drunk, and I'm the wife of a policeman. If you don't be-

53

have, she says, I'll call my husband. He'll take you to the station house. Would you want that? The peasant, afraid to be caught drunk, sold her a wonderful goose for thirty kopeks. And such a goose— fat, sly, important looking — exactly like our sergeant! Yes, brother, my wife is a treasure. Now, if you could find one like her, it would be a blessed event. She would take you in hand, and how! You wouldn't dare open your mouth!"

"What's so good about that?" Arefi asked in a knowing manner.

"What's so good about it? A woman! There's a different spirit in the house when there's a woman. For one thing, children begin coming right away; the house gets cleaned; then, there's someone to swear at and to make up with. . . ."

And there followed an endless listing of the remarkable attributes of women. Mikhailo had a unique point of view which made even the defects of women appear worthy. Women were his beloved passion, competing strongly with his other passion —food. Women were the alpha and omega of his existence, the cement that bound all the various manifestations of life into one solid whole. For him they were a power, giving everything tone, color and essence. He could talk about women in a lofty tone for three hours at a stretch. His lyrical phrases distressed Arefi who would droop sadly, lower and lower, as if trying to crawl under the table away from his friend's speech. Finally, his patience exhausted, he would rise and snarl:

"Let me be! That's enough. You can pull the soul out of a man!"

This retort stopped the orator short, but did not confound him to the point of silence. Oh, no! He would look around a bit, and then harp on the same old thing again.

"You ought to whitewash your stove. Just look at your stove! Phui! Phui! A disgrace, that's what it is. Now, if you had a woman . . ."

But Arefi would only cough and shift a leg or an arm to show his irritation.

"Don't be angry, brother! You just wait; you'll come to it yet. It just isn't possible for a man like you to be wasted. . . ."

"Mike! Stop!" Arefi's fist banged on the table.

"All right. No more. The devil take you!"

Several minutes of silence.

"I'm going home. I'm due on my beat soon. Marya must be waiting. Oh, what a supper we have to-day! Sow belly stuffed with minced meat and buckwheat kasha and fatback. The whole thing smothered in gravy. You bite into it, and it runs out of your mouth. Oh! And what filth you eat here!

What kind of eating is that? But if you had. . . . All right, no more, no more. I'll keep quiet. . . . I'm going already, I'm going. Good-by. I'm off. Come to see me sometime. And where is Paul? Paul, you little devil, where are you? He's not here, it seems. How is he? All right? He lives on the street, I suppose. Ah, what kind of a life is that for Paul? But if you had a woman. . . ."

And finally he would leave, to the accompaniment of Arefi's disgruntled mumbling. For a long time after Mikhailo's visit he would feel upset. Unpleasant currents of air seemed to be all around him.

Mikhailo's conversations were almost always the same. Paul soon learned to guess the end of his every sentence upon hearing the first words. He did not like Mikhailo's shaven, greasy face, nor his dull eyes resembling two silver buttons, nor his self-satisfied bass voice—nor his whole coarse figure with its short legs and arms and its square, closely-cropped head. Watching Mikhailo and observing Arefi's attitude toward him, Paul came to despise the epicure and to avoid him. For this he received the nickname of "Little Dodger." Paul felt that Uncle Arefi, despite his black beard, powerful figure and stern, terrifying silence, was a beauty compared with Mikhailo.

Paul could not himself draw any conclusions from the conversation of the two friends, but he always sided with Arefi. He did not trust the garrulous Mikhailo. Gradually Paul adopted Arefi's attitude toward women. He even tried to demonstrate on Tulka. At first this surprised her. Then she became angry. Finally, Paul came home with a scratched face and a secret respect for women.

Arefi asked him briefly, in a very deep voice:

"What's this?"

"I fell—against a plank," Paul answered, blushing.

"Oh. . . ." said Arefi in an indefinite tone and told him to wash up.

The days went by and Paul grew.

He was now nine years old; small, very pockmarked, clumsy, silent. His eyes were unchildlike in their coldness and wisdom. He and Arefi understood each other remarkably well. They were able to speak eloquently to each other even in their silence. Arefi taught Paul how to read and write. An attempt to send the boy to a parish school ended sadly. Paul could not stand the attitude of the boys at school for more than ten days. On the eleventh day, wakened by Arefi with the words "Get up, time for school," he raised his head from the pillow and, peering into Arefi's face with eyes inflamed by a sleepless night, made his first long speech since the day of his birth:

"I ain't going there no more, even if you drown me. I'm treated worse than a dog there. All they do is call me a bastard, a foundling, a pock-marked devil. I won't go, no matter what you do. I'd rather stay home. I don't like them. I don't like anybody. I'll always fight them. The day before yesterday I smashed the teacher's son's nose for him. The teacher made me kneel for an hour. I'll smash him again, I'll smash everybody. Go ahead, punish me! When they hit me, nobody get's blamed. I keep quiet, so nobody else has to kneel. I'm not going any more, no matter what!"

Arefi looked at the pock-marked, child face, now still more marred by discontent and venom. He was silent. But when Paul finished talking and had again pushed his face, still stubborn and challenging, into the pillow, Arefi exploded, briefly, but in such a way that the glass shook in the windows: "Don't go then!" And he looked in the direction of the school with such emotion that Paul trembled and ducked under the blanket.

Nothing further was ever mentioned about school. Laborious study went on at home. Paul did not like to study and sat down to his books as to a difficult, unpleasant task. Although Arefi's intentions were of the best he could not breathe life into dead letters and words.

Each day, after the morning tea, Paul, frowning, would take his books down from the shelf. He would sit at the table, elbows pressed to knees, chin in the palms of his hands, and begin to mumble something indistinct and unmusical, rocking back and forth, and from side to side.

The only result of this occupation was that it silenced the birds in the cages. They would exchange anxious, worried glances. Then, suddenly, at the signal of the energetic bullfinch, they would begin to whistle and chirp in various keys, as if prompted by a wicked intention to divert the boy's attention from the pursuit of learning. In this they quickly succeeded.

Paul would lift his eyes from the book and begin to whistle quietly, at first to the bullfinch, the good singer. In a short time, he would begin to tease the bird with an unpleasant whistle. Then he would upset the other finches by scraping the edge of one knife against another. Finally, when an unbelievable rumpus had been raised in the house, he would get up on the bench and occupy himself with the starling.

It was done in this way: He would poke a stick into the cage and rap the starling on the beak, a process which always annoyed the bird. The starling would jump clumsily all around the cage on one leg,

59

LIBRARY
SOUTHERN SEMINARY

flapping his wings and trying to catch the confounded splinter with his beak. But even when he did, he would soon lose it again and sink into silence, totally uninterested in the piece of wood. When he could not catch the wood, his shrieks would become more and more deafening.

At this, Paul, satisfied, would return to his books; but not to look at them. He would stare straight in front of him as if he could see through the wall. And the more he engaged in this, the more calm, deep and thoughtful his glance would become. What he thought about he scarcely understood himself. Some thoughts are devoid of shape or form, leading us to believe that we can escape by dismissing them as unimportant. But this is not so, for such a course carries within it the germ of cowardice and incipient stupidity.

Paul would sit thus in the midst of the constant chattering of the birds for two hours. Then Arefi would come in and ask about the lesson. Paul would calmly seat himself on the bench. Firmly pressing his finger on a line in the book, he would pour forth the following wisdom:

"You sew with a sew . . ."

"Wait a minute!" Arefi would interrupt. "It can't be that." And, picking up the book, he would begin to read to himself, his lips moving soundlessly.

"That's not it! Come on, now, read it again."

"You sew with a saw, and you sew with a needle."

"Well, come, now. It says *saw* there, doesn't it? What do we do with a saw?"

"With a saw?" Paul would look up at the ceiling and try to imagine. "You saw wood."

"There, you see! And you read *sew*. You see it's an *a*, not an *e*."

"But there's nothing in the book about wood."

Arefi briefly considered how he could shove aside the wood which stood in the way of successful scholarship. Paul sat back, and said:

"I know all this. We sew with a needle, we chop wood with an ax, we write with a pen, but I can't read this stuff. The words are much too small. And they're all different kinds."

Arefi pondered in silence. Looking into the book, he re-read the simple sentences and his opinion would waver. He would doubt their value in the development of a child. Then, reading further, he would be amazed at the wisdom of the writer. Arefi was sure the author would have been distressed by Paul's proposition that you sew with a saw and you saw with a needle.

In this way the hour of the lesson would pass. Arefi would give Paul homework to review the past lessons and something else "from this point to this point." Then both of them, in a sweat from their learning, would sit down to dinner. After dinner, Arefi would lie down for a nap. He would order Paul to wake him immediately if anything came up.

Paul would dress and go out into the street. He was in a continual state of war with the street. Children of his own age were not attracted by his silent, morose character. He himself, though secretly envious of their gaiety and games, made no effort to meet them halfway. Several attempts to establish friendly relations had been made, but all of them ended, for one reason or another, in Homeric battles and mutual animosity. Paul could not enter lightly into their games. He regarded everything much too deliberately and in a grownup fashion. This made an unpleasant and cold impression on other children. Paul felt that they avoided him.

Once the children had gone to the forest for mushrooms. Paul loved the melancholy sounds of the peaceful forest; they made him feel warm and soft. He broke away from his companions unnoticed. Wandering amidst the trees, his head bent as if searching for something, he hummed a song. He enjoyed the warm, luscious smell of mouldy leaves, the rustling of the grass under his feet, and the busy scurrying of small insects. . . . From afar voices reached him:

"And where's the foundling?" someone shouted.

"Who needs him? He won't get lost. No such luck!"

"He's always puffed up like an owl, like Arefi . . ."

"Maybe the cop is his real father!"

The children snickered loudly.

A cold darkness descended on Paul. Feeling insulted, he carefully stole out of the forest. Soon his sense of insult changed into fury. He wanted to get revenge and he felt justifed in doing so.

When he reached the fringe of the forest, he shouted at the top of his lungs in an excited, gay voice:

"Hey, you, kids, come quick! Look what I found!"

When in answer to his call, two children ran up, he threw himself upon them and beat them up. All the way back to town, the children held their distance, swearing and jeering at Paul, but fearing to come close. He was strong. It was dangerous to get into an open fight with him. They had learned that from more than one experience.

Paul reached home. He was sad. Arefi was out. Evening came; it was dark and quiet in the house. Only the chaffinch and the greenfinch, recently acquired and not yet settled down, violated the silence. They attracted Paul's attention. He looked at them for a long time as they jumped in their cage, pushing their heads through the wire bars. Suddenly he jumped nimbly on a chair, took the cage off the hook and, opening the little door, shoved the cage against the open window. The birds flew off. Paul did not bother to follow their flight. Distracted, he sat down again at the table, head on arm, thinking. . . .

When Arefi came in, Paul greeted him with:

"I let the birds out." He was impudent. There was challenge in his eyes.

Arefi looked around at the walls, then at Paul, and asked, briefly:

"What for?"

"Just because!" Paul answered, the same impudence in his voice and eyes.

"Well . . . that's your affair."

"And why don't you scold me?" Paul demanded.

Arefi raised his brows and mustaches. He looked kindly into the child's face.

"Have I ever scolded you?" He was sad, and began to smooth his knee with the palm of his hand.

"That's the whole trouble. Everybody else does. Maybe you ought to, too. It's all the same now."

64

Arefi fidgeted on the bench, confused. Paul had the look of an embittered man.

A depressing, heavy silence reigned. Even the birds seemed to be cowed and listened, waiting to see what would come next. But nothing happened, except that Paul gathered his feet up under him and leaned back against the wall.

The dirty old clock, with its yellow, fly-specked face, ticked off the seconds which dropped monotonously into the abyss of eternity. The clock seemed to be terribly tired of this enforced labor. The pendulum swung lazily back and forth, making a swishing sound which caused a cockroach, sitting on the wall, to wiggle its whisker ridiculously. The red rays of the glaring sun beat through the elder bushes into the window of the hut, throwing shimmering spots of light on the floor.

"So you let the birds out—that's nothing. A bird that beats about in the cage should be let out. And if it's so tame it wants to stay, then let it stay. Such a bird is no longer a bird. A good bird always yearns for freedom."

Paul looked up at Arefi.

"What are you saying that for?"

"Just so . . . nothing. . . . Just came to me, so I said it," Arefi answered, confused, pulling at his beard and feeling guilty. "One doesn't always say what one thinks. Sometimes, you twirl about your own thoughts, you twirl about, and you lose them; they break into bits . . . and that which is broken, just is no more."

"Well?" Paul asked again, his head thrust forward in attention.

"Well, nothing. Oh, it's hard to talk. Come on, Paul, let's read about the life of St. Alexis."

"Let's."

Paul lay on the bench, disappointed. He felt something new in Arefi's words; and there were so many words. That in itself was news.

Arefi took some tattered books from the shelf. Selecting one, he placed it on the table. In a few minutes, his deep bass filled the house. As his interest in the book grew, his voice deepened. Finally, it quavered down an octave lower. At times like these, Paul loved to lie with eyes closed and mentally illustrate the book with various pictures. He imagined all the saints as small and thin, with tremendous, stern, shining eyes; the martyrs, as healthy peasants in red shirts, with rolled up sleeves and squeaky boots; the emperors, persecutors of the Christians, as short legged, fat landlords who are so often very hot, which is why they are bad tempered. He imagined real faces; the priest from the monastery, the clerks from the nearby butcher shops, and police ser-

66

geant Gogolev. Paul would take the most prominent traits of their characters and the most outstanding features of their appearance and embellish them until they lost all human likeness and became ogres, frightening the creator himself with their monstrosity.

Terror of his own combination of pictures would make Paul open his eyes and look around the room, frightened. Directly in front of him, there would be Arefi's ragged head, casting enormous, fantastic shadows on the wall. The whole house would resound with his bass drone. Distinct words and phrases would break through his deep, powerful sighs. Occasionally, Paul would hear them, but he could not understand how these simple words could create such terrible pictures of martyrdom. He could not understand why, on hearing these words, he was able to see the pictures they described. He would begin to day-dream and lose the thread of the story. Sunk in his own thoughts, he would fall asleep. Opposite him, there was Arefi, completely oblivious to everything going on around him. Arefi would always read the book right to the end. For a long time afterward, he would stare as if reading something on the blank pages of the cover. Then he would sigh, glance around, get up, walk over to Paul, take him in his arms with extreme care, and carry him to his little bed behind the stove. Then, making the sign of the cross over him, he would go and sit on the bench outside the hut.

There he would gaze long and attentively at the river, the dark walls of the forest, and the starlit skies. He would listen to the dying noise of the town and look suspiciously at passing women. He would shout to the cabmen in a stern tone "Quiet, you devil!" if they drove noisily, and even more sternly, "Well, you, crawl on!" if they drove quietly. There was really no need for this shouting, but Arefi could not let one cabman pass without it. They seemed terrible ne'er-do-wells and lazybones to him. They lived by the strength of their horses whom Arefi considered so much better and wiser than their masters —at least they did not use foul language.

Sometimes a troika, bells jingling, would trot past Arefi. The driver would whoop, the women would chatter; there would be husky, drunken laughter from the men. Arefi would leap to his feet, burning with a desire to take the whole gang to the station house. His stern glance would follow them for a long time.

From the time Paul was six and began to play on the street, Arefi treated the other children harshly. He soon managed to earn their enmity. He could not reconcile himself to the fact that they would dare to treat his Paul so stupidly and so cruelly. In the beginning he did not want to believe it. Accidentally, however, he once overheard two or three epithets concerning his adopted son. Then he was convinced. No one else loved his Paul.

Unaware how it had come about, he entered into a cruel, undeclared war with the children. He permitted no noise and play on the street. His petty persecution of the children was ridiculous. At last, he became convinced that he was dealing not with children, as might appear on the surface, but with young people who had already acquired all the stupid feelings and prejudices of adults.

This conviction often brought Arefi into sharp friction with the residents of the town. During such clashes he was forced, more than once, to listen to many unpleasant accusations against Paul. Always, after such bouts, he would become even more gloomy. His whole face would become deeply wrinkled, his eyes would gleam in a disturbed, nervous way. His face seemed to retreat behind his beard, mustaches and brows.

When he read his beloved lives of the saints, his voice would deepen. Sometimes it would begin to quiver with a strange, metallic ring.

Paul's relationship with Arefi remained the same —there was the same silence between them. Arefi's speech was rare and stilted. He spoke to the boy as he spoke to everyone — except cab-drivers and women. His ordinary conversation was almost diffident in tone. In this tone, he reported to the sergeant, gave orders to janitors, coaxed drunks to go home and answered the questions of passers-by who rarely approached him; his forbidding large figure and face hidden in the dense black beard did not encourage inquiry.

As time went on he sat less and less in his hut. Even at night, when it was unnecessary to keep watch, he used to go out and sit on the bench under the elder bushes.

Motionless as a stump, he would sit until dawn. Sometimes he would fall aseep there. But usually, he stared at the field beyond the river, not tearing his eyes away from a chosen point. Sometimes he would get up and go down to the river; he would sit on the stones as if listening for something. The river rolled on into the distance, quietly, quietly whispering something to the shore. . . .

As Paul grew older, he too retreated more and more into himself, became ever more morosely quiet. He was too much so for children his own age. He no longer tried to establish a relationship with them, remembering that former attempts had yielded him more grief than pleasure.

After one such effort, he had entered the house upset, his teeth clenched, black and blue marks under his eyes, his lips bloody.

"Fighting again?" Arefi asked, rather coaxingly. "Oh, brother, you're a warrior, always fighting!"

Paul sat on the bench in silence, sucked his lip and spat. He never ran to Arefi with complaints and tears. He settled his own accounts with his enemies in his own way. He never let anyone get away with anything, and he never cried. Arefi liked that.

"And who did you run into this time? Tulka? Eh?"

At any other time Arefi would not have said anything further. But now, seeing that Paul was stung to the quick about something, he made an effort to draw him out. He did not have to make too many overtures; Paul's head dropped down and, in a dull shaking voice, he said:

"Where's my father and mother?"

Arefi, busying himself in front of the stove, straightened up as if Paul were the police sergeant. His eyes opened wide, he stared at the bent figure in terror. Paul did not see Arefi's attitude and face. He waited for an answer for a long time, but none came.

"What kind of people were they?" Paul lifted his head and in a twisted fashion, not like a child, smiled at the tired and frightened face of Arefi.

Arefi recovered himself.

"Your mother was the skin of a drum, and your father—a rogue!" he roared, filling the entire house with his thunderous voice and substantiating his opinion of Paul's parents with such swearing as the boy had never before heard from him, and was never to hear again.

Paul drooped and was quiet.

Arefi sat on the bench, paying no attention to the pot which boiled over on the stove, pouring water on the sizzling wood. There was an uneasy, long silence.

Paul finally asked timidly: "Did you know them?"

"Yes. . . ." Arefi hissed. "Why shouldn't I know them! The mere fact that they threw their child under a fence proves what they were—no good!"

"And are they alive?"

"Well, that I don't know . . . I guess they're done for. She probably died of grief over you—and he, he drank himself to death—or something like that . . . also by a fence . . . most probably, and died, —like a dog."

"And you—have you seen them?"

"Never have I seen such trash in my whole life! Have I seen them?"

Paul gathered that if Arefi had seen his parents,

it would not have gone well with them. He understood, and he never again returned to this dark subject. Arefi himself talked about it only once, as if moved by some sort of mysterious, somewhat romantic idea.

"It's plain that you are not the son of simple, common people. Your brain isn't common — and things like that. Not common."

It is hard to say how Arefi came to the conclusion that Paul was the son of complex and worldly people. Paul did not give him any basis for such a deduction. No one guessed that he loved the child; this was Arefi's secret. Aside from this one time, the question of Paul's lineage was never again raised.

Did Paul think of it? Perhaps. He thought of so much that certainly he could not have left this question unexplored.

The fantasy of man has few limits. The fantasy of a child has even fewer boundaries, for the soul of a child is much more mysterious than the soul of an adult; it is free from these petty traits so evident in a grown man who has yielded to the temptations of life.

4

Once, returning from his beat, Arefi noticed the starling acting very strangely. He sat motionless in his cage. Then he suddenly flew from the perch, landing upside down. He fell into the cup of water several times. Then he would shake himself thoroughly, click his bill and flap his wings. After such a drop, he returned to his perch only with great effort, although previously he had been able to fly there easily. When he finally got back to the perch, he did not sit in the middle of it as he had once done, but huddled up against the side wall of the cage.

On this particular day, the crippled bird flapped his wings in his peculiar manner, trying to support himself on the perch with one leg. But apparently it was very difficult for him to hold on.

"The cripple's going to die," Arefi told Paul, looking critically at the bird.

"No!" exclaimed Paul, who liked the starling more than any of the other birds.

"I'm afraid so. He's too old."

"Don't touch him. Leave him alone."

Paul looked sadly at the bird which was swaying more and more vigorously on his perch.

"Maybe we should take him out into the air?" Arefi suggested.

"I suppose so."

So they took the cage off the hook and brought it out to the elder bushes in front of the house. It was a bright day in March, the sun's rays shone on the puddles of water, the crumbly snow was melting, and the horizon was wide open and temptingly free of the gray mass of wintry clouds. Beyond the river there was a broad, winding black-brown strip of road. On both sides of it, bright patches of thawing earth glistened in the sun. The sky was clear and the young spring sun shone gaily.

But all this could not enliven the starling. He

looked around sedately, shook his head, whistled softly and long, then fell from the perch—and died just as Paul was about to open the small door of the cage, take the bird out and place it on the grass.

The boy stepped back quickly and looked on in pity as the bird's leg was drawn out in the death spasm. When the bird finally shuddered and became still, the tears rolled down Paul's cheeks. Taking the bird from the cage, he turned it about in his hands; his tears dripped on its feathers.

"So, you can cry! That means you will cry when I die," Arefi said quietly, bending over the boy.

Paul threw the bird to the ground and, clasping his arms around Arefi's neck, buried his head in Arefi's breast, murmuring incoherently through his shaking sobs.

"Now, now. Don't cry. It'll be all right. There are still some good people in this world. You'll survive. Only it'll be hard for you; you're too stiff. You don't yield. You don't bow. That's the sad part of it. But then again if you bend, it's twice as bad, because then everybody will walk all over you—saddle and ride you. But it'll be all right. You'll come through. The important thing is—study!"

Arefi's harsh, axe-like words quieted Paul. Together they arranged a funeral. They dug a little hole among the roots of the elder bushes, lined it with small shells and sprinkled it with earth.

Paul, greatly affected by this incident, asked Arefi's permission to place a cross on the bird's grave. He busied himself planing one from a small piece of wood, while Arefi, deep in weighty thoughts which furrowed his forehead, sat in a corner on the bench and watched Paul from under his brows.

"I have an idea I'll die soon. Sometimes I feel very bad. So you'd better listen close."

Paul laid his knife on the table and listened attentively.

"First of all, Mikhailo has thirty-five rubles and twenty kopeks of mine. He owes me that. Then there's seventeen and a half rubles in my trunk. I won't give them to you; I'll take them to the post-office where there is a savings bank. I'll get a little yellow book for the money. You take care of that book. Later, I'm going to get you into a shop. Oh, Paul, it'll be rotten for you there! Yes, pretty bad. People can be such dogs! They drink, they swear, they're libertines—it won't be a picnic for you. They'll beat you. They'll abuse you. . . . Ech!"

Arefi rose with a sharp movement, took his cap from the hook, put it on his head and walked out of the house. Paul went back to making the cross for the grave of the deceased starling. He was oppressed by the prophesy of Arefi's death.

When Arefi returned to the hut late that night, Paul was already asleep. Arefi never again mentioned the subject of his death.

Another two months passed. Suddenly Paul had a tremendous desire to learn. He would sit at his books for days on end, but book learning came to him with difficulty. Frequently, he lost patience with his books. His face sweating, he would try to make out some word, and then suddenly discover that he had known that word all along. This would infuriate him. He would put the question to himself: Why are such words written here?

Once, angry at his studies, he announced to Arefi that all books were written for spite and that there was nothing in them that he, Paul, needed.

"And what do you need?" Arefi asked.

"I?" Paul considered. "Well, it says here: 'Children, it is late. The clock, too, reads two to two.' And further on, it says: 'Ward, cord, war, word, curd, were!' What do I need that for?"

"Yes, it does seem kind of mixed up. But go on, read more."

Paul read on and still was not satisfied. He could not find the answers to the confusing questions in his mind. On that day, he finished reading two stories and, as usual, in a bewildered fashion, questioned: What's the good of all this?

The distant shouts and laghter of the boys reached him. A merry sun pushed into the window of the hut. Paul became ever more infuriated. He could not concentrate on his books. The birds chirped energetically, hopping in their cages. Paul, glancing sidewise at them, remembered how once he had wanted to free all the birds. Somewhere in the distance there was the heavy rumble of an approaching carriage. Paul looked out the window. A baker passed by on the street and he realized he was hungry. For some reason, Arefi was a long time getting home that day.

The carriage rumbled closer and closer to the house; now it came round the corner. A policeman sat in it. But not Arefi. It was Mikhailo. Why he? thought Paul, and walking out, stood at the door. Even from that distance, Mikhailo was waving his hands, as if calling to him. Paul saw that he was unusually dishevelled. His cap was cocked to one side and sat far back on his head; his coat was unbuttoned. Paul realized that something must have happened.

"Hurry, quick, get in!" Mikhailo shouted. "Back to the hospital!" he ordered, poking the cabman in the back.

"Wh-a-t — happened?" Paul cried, paling. He pulled at Mikhailo's sleeve.

"Something bad. Arefi's gone mad. His mind's all tangled up. He went crazy. Understand? He came to the sergeant and said, 'Torture me, I'm a Christian. Torture me, I don't want to talk to you. I don't want to have anything to do with you.' Gogolev smacked him in the teeth, but he paid no attention. 'Go on, hit me,' he says. 'Dioscuri, I shall remain a Christian unto eternity.' My God, what nonsense! Then Arefi began to pull things off the shelves, throw them on the floor and stamp on them. 'I'll crush your idols into the dust,' he says, and things like that. Well, of course, they immediately tied him up and took him to the hospital, and he kept on talking and talking. Oh, yes! there you have it. It's those books coming out. It's only grief that learning brings. You get to thinking, and all that's no good comes into your head. Right away it's how and why and what for and—phui! You go out of your mind! It's a great pity, it is. Why, he's my old friend."

Paul sat oppressed, gloomy, pale. He listened quietly, remembering Arefi as he had seen him yesterday, the day before yesterday, and before that, all the days in the depths of the past. He had noticed nothing unusual about the old policeman, except

81

perhaps that he was becoming thinner from day to day; his eyes had been sinking deeper and deeper; his glance, usually stolid and gloomy, had recently become somewhat shifty, sometimes glistening unnaturally as if in joy, and sometimes as if in fear of something that stood before him.

Once, and it was not long before, he had talked about life in Tashkent, of the heat, of the sand, of the wild people there and of something they had done for which they had to be killed like rats. But, having spoken about that, he had again lapsed into silence, and from then on, until this very morning, he had been his old self.

"And won't he get better?" Paul interrupted Mikhailo's philosophical oration.

"He? Well, it's—understood. Sure he'll get well. And as for the doctor—how can he possibly know what will happen? Never! A doctor can heal and that's all. More than that he cannot do. Did you lock the door? Driver, stop! Is the door locked, eh?"

"Did the doctor really say something? Tell me, did he? Oh, why did you stop the driver? Let's go. Hurry. Hurry, Uncle Mikhailo!"

"What do you mean, let's go? When the hut's open! What a guy! Let's go, he says. Why, they'll clean out the place. Driver, turn back! Go back, you fool!"

"Dear Uncle Mikhailo! Let's not. Let's go there, to Uncle Arefi. The hut can go to the dogs!" Paul shouted, upset.

"That's impossible, you funny kid. I'll go back myself. Myself. . . . Driver, go ahead, take him to the hospital. Well, get going! Go to the crazy house. And you, Paul, when you get there, you ask. . . ."

But the carriage rumbled on just then and Paul did not hear what he was supposed to ask. He fidgeted, and kept prodding the driver: "Go faster!"

"We'll get there soon," the driver answered in a confident tone. He smacked his lips, waved his whip in the air, and scolded the horse, shouting: "Well, where're you going, you fool? Have you too gone mad?" And, pulling the reins, he turned the horse's head first to the right and then to the left, to which she replied with an indignant swish of her sparse tail and a discontented snort.

Mikhailo's sad news seemed to have freed Paul's mind from the enveloping cloud in which he had lived till then. For the first time, he was able to see the reality around him. Instinctively, he was on the alert, suspicious, distrustful. He tried with all his strength to stifle the ever-growing, heartbreaking grief welling up in him. Now he felt alone, defenseless.

Everything—the driver, the street, the people

walking about, now appeared to him much stranger than they had yesterday; they aroused in him a frightening apprehension of something offensive and undesirable. Even the bright summer sky, that yesterday had been warm and caressing, to-day appeared heartless and indifferent, having no kinship with Paul.

"Do you think he'll get better?" he asked the driver as they drew up to a wire fence. Behind it stood the yellow hospital building; cold and forbidding.

"Him? He'll get we-e-ll. To the left, you devilish doll, to the left! What a good-for-nothing nag!"

But before the devilish doll managed to turn left, Paul had jumped off the carriage and sped like an arrow to a dark spot in the yellow wall.

Paul was swallowed by the yawning door. Where to go now?

"What do you want?" someone asked from somewhere.

Paul mumbled hurriedly, his head down trying not to look at whoever was talking to him:

"A policeman—crazy—to-day, he was brought here—show me—where is he?"

"Oh! Go straight ahead, straight ahead. Who is he—your father?"

Paul raised his head. A broad back in a red shirt moved before him.

"Is he your father?" this figure repeated in a tenor voice, not turning to face Paul. Suddenly, the figure stopped so abruptly and unexpectedly that Paul's face pushed into its back.

"Here, Nicholas Nicholaevich, is the son of the policeman."

A gentleman in glasses walked up to Paul and took him by the chin.

"Well, what do you want, boy?" he asked gently and quietly.

Paul glanced up at him in surprise. This gentleman's face was thin, pale, small.

"What do you want then, eh?"

"I'd like to see him . . ."

"You can't do that—you can't."

Paul's face wrinkled up; he began to cry softly. His head whirled.

"Then how am I going to . . ." he asked through his tears.

But the gentleman was no longer there. There was only the man in a red shirt and a white apron. He stood before Paul, his hands behind his back, biting his lip, thoughtfully watching the boy. Paul pressed firmly against the wall and whimpered.

"No, now. Come with me, quickly, so the doctor

won't see. Well, come," and, grasping Paul's hand, he rushed him toward the end of the corridor.

"Look!"

Paul was seized from behind, lifted into the air, and shoved against a round glass set in the door behind which Arefi's powerful bass voice droned.

Arefi stood in the middle of the room in a long white gown, his arms tightly twisted behind his back. A long nightcap hung down his back. His face and head were shaven; this made his large ears appear to be bulging out. His cheeks had turned yellow and were sunken; his cheekbones sharp. His eyes were open wide and deeply sunken into black pits, and under one there was a red bruise. From a little red star immediately noticeable on the left cheek, trickled drops of blood which made a thin ribbon cutting across his cheek, extending over his neck, and becoming lost in the collar of his gown. Arefi was horribly thin and tall.

"You have forced me into the dungeon!" he droned, his eyes glistening terribly. "I suffer in the name of my God and shall suffer unto eternity. But I have destroyed your idols and have turned your altars into dust. I have turned your altars into dust. It is because that ye have not torn out my tongue that I accuse you, sinners! You have forgotten the God of Truth, and ye wander in the darkness, you stagnate badly. Anathema, anathema, anathema. You corrupt the souls of the young. You shall have no salvation. You are wreckage. Fragments. You have tortured me. Why have ye tortured me? And beaten me? It is for the Truth, for the God who is in my heart. . . ."

His deep voice in turn thundered and lowered to a whisper, to a sad, soft whisper, which made Paul shudder as if in fever and push back in fright from the small window.

"I await my death, you heathens. I await my glory. Where are the hangmen and the persecutors? Anathema, anathema, anathema!"

Wild, terrible shouts shook the door, the glass through which Paul was looking vibrated.

"Well, that's enough, now. Go home quickly. Go, or the doctor will see you."

To the accompaniment of Arefi's shouts, Paul walked down the corridor and out, in a stupor. Arefi's curses thundered in his ears, his terrible whisper resounded. Arefi's angular, yellow shaven face seemed to enlarge to tremendous proportions, his eyes became gigantic as the sun, and shone as brightly, but it was a black, gloomy shining. Then it suddenly divided itself into many small faces, sprinkling gradually before Paul's eyes, penetrating his heart with a thousand sharp glances and filling it with increasingly heavy despair and grief.

Various pictures of his past life with Arefi appeared—when he was healthy, bearded, silent. These pictures would appear and disappear, be replaced by other pictures, and they, too, would disappear. The boy's mind was caught in a whirlwind. Now the past flashed before him; then suddenly he was plunged into a strange darkness—without thought, without image. Again there opened before him a chain of past episodes, in no proper sequence. He felt grief and dull pain when he recalled them. His pity for Arefi, his fear for himself, a whole chaos of feelings interchanged one with the other, fused, became a stone crushing his head, his shoulders, his chest.

The river was before him. The cold blew from it. Dark and whispering, entirely cloaked by the night, it flowed on in the distance and lost itself. Over it was the sky, thickly covered with ragged, torn clouds. Two or three small stars glistened from among the chunks of broken clouds. The whole sky was torn, old; it seemed ready to fall to the ground, and into the calm, dreamy river which, in its dark waves, reflected the pitiful, poor, blue fragments of the heavens and the lonely stars. Beyond the river, the horizon had become dark and terribly quiet.

Paul ran back to the hut. But it was locked. He

stood still for a while, then he lay down beside the elder bushes, face up, watching the clouds crawl slowly across the sky, until he fell asleep—a heavy sleep filled with nightmares.

5

Paul was awakened by strong jabs in the back. He opened his eyes for a moment. Then he had to close them to avoid the sun which was beating down directly upon his head. In that moment, he saw a familiar face bent over him.

Immediately he remembered everything.

"Well, get up!" a woman's voice rang out over him.

He rose quickly. There was Marya, looking at him with kindly curiosity.

"Come to my house. Poor thing! Look where you've slept! Why didn't you come to us for the night?"

Paul did not answer. He did not like Marya. He didn't like her because she was so large and strong, because she swore so much, because her eyes were gray, her voice chesty and coarse. In fact, he didn't like any part of her energetic, eternally watchful, pugnacious personality.

They went off together.

"Well, now, don't you go killing yourself. It'll be all right. God and good people will help you. You'll survive. Just be on the lookout. Watch, be sharp, understand what's what. Learn to live — though that's a difficult thing to do. You've always got to be on the lookout. Otherwise, you'll stay a fool. Perhaps this was all for the best. What did you get from Arefi? No real attention, no learning. Only pampering. He treated you just as if you were grown up. Now is that a way to do? You're a child, and one must treat you like a child. And he himself, if we're going to be frank about it, was a fool of fools.

"One must live, and he kept on reading books. What sort of wisdom is it to read books? You have to live your life, and get along with other people! Get strong, get to be respected, that's much more important than all your books! He worked as a policeman for eleven years and nothing to show for it!"

Paul listened angrily and only muttered in disapproval of Marya's militant philosophy. But when she swore at Arefi and called him a fool, he pulled at her dress boldly, as if wishing to halt further references to his guardian. But she, carried away by her own eloquence, did not notice and continued passionately:

"Don't you trust others. If they caress you, it's a lie. If they praise you, it's a lie. But when they swear at you, then they're not lying, even if they overdo it. The important thing is to be cautious with everyone. Stop and think—isn't he trying to get something out of me? And when you see he isn't, then you can make a step forward. But even then you've got to be careful. Don't trust your own judgment. You've got to be as suspicious of yourself sometimes as you would be of a stranger. Because a man doesn't always know what's good for himself. He thinks, 'that's it,' but no, he's way off. Then he finds himself right in the middle of a mess!"

Interested in her own reasoning, Marya quite forgot to whom she was speaking, and began to discuss things in great detail, until she reached the point at which she announced suddenly:

"And you watch out when it comes to women!"

93

Here her glance fell accidentally on her audience. He trotted beside her, with short steps, hardly able to keep up with her sturdy, masculine stride. In his little red shirt, barefoot, his sad little pock-marked face still bearing the marks of sleep, his hair dishevelled, Paul was so childishly miserable and pitiful compared to her powerful figure.

An energetic expectoration placed a period on her lecture. All the way to her house, she said nothing further to Paul.

When they entered the corridor of the station house, Mikhailo came toward them with a pot in his hands.

"Ah, you've come! That's fine! Time for dinner, Marya, eh? Where've you been?" and turning to Paul "Where'd you sleep?"

"Over there . . . near the hut."

"What a boy!" Mikhailo said thoughtfully, walking into the room after them.

Marya had already taken off her coat and was poking up the stove.

"I've got some fresh cheese. Where shall I put it? Eh?"

"Where'd you get it?" Marya asked, brightening up. Taking the pot from her husband's hands, she poked her nose into it. "Good, fresh cheese!"

"A present from a little peasant. For a favor—"

Mikhailo explained. Slyly winking at his wife, he clicked his tongue.

"Oh, you scarecrow!" Marya pinched the back of his neck affectionately.

"What a woman! My spouse! I have something else too. But let's eat! Feed me well, woman, and I'll tell you."

"Ah, come on now," Marya wheedled, an expression of curiosity on her face.

Mikhailo shoved his hand into his pocket and jingled some change, a look of solemnity on his glossy, shaven face.

"How much?" Marya asked in a happy whisper.

"One and a half rubles, five kopeks, and a bucket of cucumbers."

"Is that all?" his wife drawled in disappointment. "There was more on Wednesday."

"Well, that was Wednesday. To-day is Friday. There are fairs and fairs. You know, to-day, that new sergeant Korpenko looked at me suspiciously. Damn him! He married two brick stores, and so much money. Suddenly he's become as pure as a new-laid egg. I should have married like that!"

"You dog! I'll marry you to this here poker!"

During this conversation, Paul stood at the door and watched them, feeling superfluous, neglected, of no concern to these people. He tried to imagine what would happen to him later on, but could not.

He interrupted the exchange of pleasantries between the two. "Will we go there soon?"

"Where? Where?" Mikhailo said turning to him.

"To the hospital."

"Why should you be going there? Are you crazy? Sit down there on the bunk and wait. We'll have dinner soon. Our kids will be back from school soon. Then you'll play outside with them."

Paul sat on the bunk, sunk in grief, hearing and seeing nothing that went on around him. When he was called to dinner, he sat at the table but could not eat; he put down his spoon.

"What's this?" Marya asked rather severely.

"I don't want to eat," Paul answered quietly.

They took turns lecturing him. However, this did not in the least interfere with their rapid and successful emptying of the large oval tureen of soup which gave off a thick aroma of cooking fat and oversteamed cabbage.

"Anathema!" This word rang in Paul's ears in dull, metallic hammer blows.

"Anathema!" he repeated in a whisper and imagined the hollow-cheeked, mindless face of Arefi. Paul's lips moved, he shuddered. The blood drained out of his face, then rushed back in a hot wave. He flushed and paled alternately. The pockmarks on his cheeks and forehead turned into compact red spots.

"What's that you're mumbling there? You spotted dodger, you!" Mikhailo shouted, getting up from the table.

"I'm going," Paul said firmly and rose from the bench.

"Where to?" Marya asked sternly.

"I'm going back to the hut."

"Why there? There's a new policeman there. He doesn't know you. He'll chase you right out. Sit down here and behave yourself!"

Paul sat down. Mikhailo disappeared behind the cotton curtain draped over the bed, which creaked mournfully as he lay down.

"What about the birds?" Paul said after a moment. He looked questioningly at Marya.

Mikhailo answered from behind the curtain, "I let them all out. And I brought all your belongings here." He yawned, dreamily. "No, you see, you've no business there!"

"Where's the trunk?" Paul asked a little while later.

Mikhailo was already snoring. Marya sat at the window sewing. No one answered. Paul went into a corner and rolled up on the bunk.

"What will happen to me now?" he thought.

The river rose before his eyes, and the small sticks

that floated upon it. Some of them were driven up to the shore and remained there. Paul recalled how he always threw those back into the stream. He didn't like them because they did not want to continue on their course. He wanted them to float out to where the river was lost. Where does the river go? Into another, and together with that one, into the sea. Arefi had told him that. The sea—that's a lot of water, so much that if you go so far from the shore that you lose sight of it, you still can't see the other bank. You can't see it in a day, not in two or three. Or was that just Arefi's notion? He's crazy! Was he always crazy?

Paul sat in his corner and thought of Arefi, of the sea, and always returned to the one question—what would happen to him to-morrow?

A sharp whisper cut across his thoughts. It was apparently assumed that he was asleep. Behind their curtain, the couple were talking about him.

"He asked about the trunk," Marya said.

"Well?" Mikhailo questioned in alarm.

"Where, says he, is the trunk?"

"What a little devil!" Mikhailo said in a surprised whisper. "We better hurry and take him to Savelich quick. It's plain he knows there was some money in that trunk. Maybe, Marya, you better take him to-morrow."

"Look at him squirm. To-morrow. What a hurry he's in! He's scared, the turkey! What are you afraid of?"

"Just the same, you know, supposing he suddenly asks 'and was there money?' Hunh? What will you say then?"

"Bl-ock-he-ad!" Marya drawled sardonically. Then their whispering became so low that Paul could hear no more.

This conversation did not arouse in him any new feeling against the pair, although he understood, of course, that they were planning to rob him. But he was entirely indifferent, partly because he did not know the power of money, but more because he could think of nothing but the sad plight of Arefi, and about that mysterious to-morrow which would close the door on the life he had known.

He had never liked Marya and Mikhailo, but on this particular day his dislike grew stronger. He realized that they did not like him and did not want him. He knew he would not have to be with them for long. He thought he could not stand their company another day.

Now, as they snored in a race one with the other, they seemed even more distasteful to him than when they were awake. Sitting in his corner, swaying, he could not shake the thought of to-morrow, the to-morrow of which he knew nothing.

Yawns and groans came from behind the curtain. Mikhailo, head dishevelled, face wrinkled with sleep, stumbled out into the room.

He turned to Paul. "Sleeping?"

"No!"

"Did my kids come?"

"No!"

"No, and no. That's your only answer! Well, I guess they went to their aunt in the village. Time to put up the samovar. Have to go on my beat pretty soon."

He went off into the corridor.

Then Marya lazily got out of bed. She stared at Paul, then began to comb her hair. Her braids were thick, chestnut, and he thought, how young she is, not one gray hair. But you take Arefi, he was very gray.

"Well, Paul, what are you thinking about? How you're going to live?" Marya suddenly asked, turning to face him, and grimacing because the comb, instead of slipping through her hair, was tearing it.

"I don't know." Paul shook his head.

"So-o-o!" Marya drawled. "And who should know? You little dope, you!"

She sighed and stopped talking. Paul, too, said

nothing. This continued until Mikhailo brought in the boiling samovar. They sat at the table and drank tea in silence.

"Well, fellow!" Marya finally began, pouring herself a third cup of tea. She had already managed to become so hot and sweaty she had to unfasten the two top buttons of her blouse.

"Now, you listen to me and remember this!" she said in a solemn tone, and then paused significantly. "To-morrow I'll take you to a shoemaker, a fellow I know. You'll be an apprentice. Be good, don't fool around, work, learn, pay attention to the boss and the workmen. Then you'll learn how to be a man. At first, it'll seem hard, but be patient. You'll get used to it. Then it'll be easy. A boy like you has no one. On holidays, you can come to us, as if we were your relatives, those who are close to you. Come, drink, eat with us. We'll always welcome you and be happy to have you. Do you understand?"

Paul understood and nodded to show he understood.

"Don't forget who took care of you. Don't forget us, I mean! And we won't forget you!" Mikhailo said as if explaining a lesson. He eyed Paul to see how the boy would react.

Paul lifted his eyes as if to ask "Why shouldn't I forget?" and then looked away.

Mikhailo sighed in disappointment and excitedly began to blow on his saucer of hot tea.

Again silence reigned. Paul looked at the pair from under his brows and felt the need and, at the same time, the right to do something to cause them some discomfort. At first he could think of nothing effective, but then he remembered.

"Where is the trunk?" he asked suddenly.

The pair looked at each other.

"I have the trunk. Don't even think about the trunk. It'll be safe here. When you grow up to be big, come and say, 'Give me my trunk.' I'll give it to you—right away! 'Here you are, Paul, here's your trunk untouched'. Yes, Yes. And whatever is in it, your pants, shirts, of course you can take those with you."

His speech ended, Mikhailo sighed deeply, his shaven face expressing both grief and apprehension.

Marya was silent, looking searchingly at Paul.

"But, there was money in it. Where did you put it?" Paul said the words very slowly.

"Money?" exclaimed Mikhailo, great surprise in his voice and on his face as he turned to Marya.

"Wife! Was there any money there? Was there money in the trunk? Eh? I didn't see any money in that trunk of yours. No, I can't say that I saw any money. May God strike me dead if I did!"

102

"What are you calling on God for, you fool? Does someone say you lie? You, you old toadstool! You haven't seen so you haven't seen! He swears by God!"

"But I only called on God as my witness, that's all! Is that a sin? The Good Book says: 'don't take the name of the Lord in vain', but this is not in vain, this is to support what I said."

Paul watched them. He saw that Mikhailo was embarrassed by his questions and did not know how to get out of the difficult situation, while Marya was not in the least concerned. The boy was furious and went on:

"There were seventeen rubles there. And you have thirty-five more. That's what! Uncle Arefi told me that. He said so not long ago."

To Paul's extreme surprise, both burst into laughter. Marya threw her head back. Her chest thrust forward, she shook with heavy, masculine guffaws, while Mikhailo choked on high, tenor giggles.

Paul did not understand. He looked at them and smiled hesitantly, as if not knowing whether to join them or not.

"Sure is funny, that Arefi! Thirty-five rubles! He certainly picked a figure!" Mikhailo sputtered through his laughter.

"Oh, you baby! Arefi told you and you believed it! What an idea *that* is! Crazy loon! Why, he's gone mad, you fool!" Marya said in mock regret, recovering from her attack of laughter.

Paul then understood the sense of their laughter. He took a deep breath, paled, then, shaking with fury, he threw in their faces:

"You lie! Both of you are lying! Don't think I didn't hear what you said in bed! I heard everything! You thieves! You, both of you are thieves! That's what! You're thieves!" To emphasize his words, Paul kicked the table.

Mikhailo was taken aback; frightened, he popped his eyes at Marya. He sat very still, his arms on the table. But Marya demonstrated immediately that she was no blunderhead.

"There you have it!" she cried out, pretending to be frightened. She jumped from her seat when Paul, through yelling, pale, agitated, sat down at his place. His eyes glistened furiously.

"Oh, my God! Oh! Mikhailo, you fool, run for the doctor! Run quick! Why, the brat's gone mad, too! You see, you see how his eyes glisten! Oh, heavenly father! It never rains but it pours! It must be a punishment for some sin! Poor, poor thing! He just couldn't stand Arefi's fate! Gone mad. Gone off his nut!"

Despite his agitation, Paul understood that he was being played for a fool. He burst into tears, bitter, angry tears. He suddenly realized that he could not cope with life and with people.

These were the first tears on the first day of his being alone in the world.

Having frightened him, they called no doctor, of course. But until he fell asleep, they took painstaking care of Paul. They put him to bed in the corner where he had spent most of the day. As he was falling asleep, he heard Marya's thick whisper:

"That boy's no fool. He's got a sharp tongue. It's a good thing he's sharp. That means he'll get along."

In his sleep, Paul saw many mischievous monsters. Ugly and huge, slimy and small, they circled round him and chuckled, clicking their teeth. Everything shook with their laughter. Paul shivered, too. In place of the sky, a large black nothingness hung over him, from which the monsters fell in groups and singly. It was very terrifying, and yet it was somehow also gay. . . .

He was awakened in the morning, given tea and taken to the shoemaker's. Paul went along indifferently. He did not feel the future held anything good for him, and in this, of course, he was not mistaken.

He was brought to a low-ceilinged, gloomy room,

where amid clouds of smoke, four human figures sang songs and tapped away with their hammers. Holding Paul by the shoulder, Marya talked with a short man who swayed from side to side, murmuring:

"Why, we have a paradise here! Not just a habitation, but a paradise! And the food—it's heavenly! Everything is just perfect. Good-by."

Marya left. Paul sat down on the floor and began to remove his boot. Something had fallen into it and was pinching his foot. Something struck his back. He looked around and saw an old boot-heel on the floor. At the door, a dirty-faced boy of his own age stuck out his tongue and hissed:

"Pock-marked face, stitched-on nose,
Devil take you where he goes!"

Paul turned away, sighed, and pulled on his boot.

"Come over here, my friend!" one of the men shouted, the one who sat on a low tub.

Paul went up to him boldly.

"Hold this!" and the man shoved a tarred waxen end of leather into his hand. "Twist it like this, boy! Twist harder!"

Paul twisted as he looked around the shop from under his gloomy brows.

And so Paul entered the ranks of labor. The shop where he worked belonged to Miron Toporkov, a fat, round man with small pig's eyes and a tremendous bald head.

He was not a bad fellow. He was mild and approached life with some humor. He had a forgiving attitude toward human foibles, although he liked to make jokes. Apparently, he had at one time read many holy books. This was reflected in his speech. But now, aside from liquor labels, he read nothing. When he was drunk he treated his help in a comradely fashion, but when he was sober he was somewhat more strict. However, he rarely gave them cause to complain. He devoted little time to the shop because of his passion for drink.

The entire responsibility for the shop lay on the shoulders of Grandfather Utkin, an old soldier with a wooden leg, a man who was straightforward both in speech and manner, a stickler for obedience and order.

Besides Grandfather Utkin, there were two assistants, Nikander Milov and Kolka Shishkin. The first had fiery red hair, was a daredevil, loved to sing, and even more to drink. He knew very well that when he slanted his merry green eyes and knitted his brows, his face became devilishly beautiful.

The second assistant was colorless and seemed

downtrodden and sickly. He had a bad and evil character. When he spoke in a caressing whisper, he was able to twist everyone to his advantage. Then he would immediately repel his listener with some sort of unexpected, absurdly cruel prank. From the second day of his apprenticeship, Paul hated Kolka.

There was the boy Artiushka. A passionate tease, always smeared with ashes, glue, and slop, he immediately entered into a sparring relationship with Paul, which soon ended in a fight. Artiushka, to his surprise, was beaten. For a week, he cast gloomy glances at Paul and tried in every way to avenge his defeat. Then, seeing that Paul was totally indifferent to all his pranks, he decided to come to terms.

"I'll tell you what, pock-mark, let's make up!" he said. "To hell with it! So you beat me up. That's because you're still healthy. But wait till you've been here a while. You'll dry up. Then I'll give you a sound beating. Agreed?"

He stretched his hand out to Paul who gave him his, without saying a word.

"Still, you ought to know that you're a junior worker here. *That* you've got to know! Since you're the junior you'll have to do all the dirty work. Understand? Agreed?"

Paul looked into the dirty face and said he agreed.

"Well!" Artiushka exclaimed, surprised. "That's

good. That's what I like! This is what it means. You clean up the shop, put up the samovar, chop the wood, heat the stove, sweep the yard, and all the rest."

"And you?"

"And I? What a funny guy you are! There'll be plenty left for me! Even more than for you."

Having established this division of labor, Artiushka was completely free of all work. For five days he smiled angelically, seeing how his dupe sweated under the burden of his duties.

But Grandfather Utkin noticed and called Artiushka to him. Smacking him over the head with a boot-tree, he said that although he was a shrewd rogue, he was not shrewd enough. Then, setting Artiushka's duties, he called to Paul, told him he was a fool and gave him his instructions too.

From that time on, there was a clear cut line between the respective duties of Paul and Artiushka. Paul was entrusted with all the dirty work, work that had nothing in common with the shoemaker's trade. Artiushka was seated on a barrel and gradually introduced into the mysteries of the trade. This immediately gave him the right to treat Paul even more imperiously. Sometimes he shouted at Paul like an official.

For a long time after that, Paul wondered just

what Grandfather Utkin had done to change the situation. Everything was just as Artiushka had arranged it. Yet Grandfather Utkin said the arrangement was his own idea.

The change from the calm, meditative existence in Arefi's hut to this life, full of swearing and singing, tobacco smoke and the smell of leather, was oppressive for Paul. Accustomed to being alone for days on end, or simply in the company of Arefi, it was only with great difficulty that he became acclimated to the constant society of the four workmen. From morning to night, these four found it easy to sing, to talk about things Paul could not understand, to laugh at one another, and, for no apparent reason, unload a tremendous quantity of murderously expressive swear words, for each of which Arefi would have hustled them off to the police station. Paul viewed his superiors gloomily and with malevolence. He could not understand them and was, therefore, a little afraid of them. Noticing his attitude, they laughed at him all the more, and at times brought him to such a pitch that his green eyes would burn with a belligerent flame. This amused them and encouraged them to go further; Paul became more and more alienated from them.

Often they would retell the story of his birth; they would make a conducted tour of it. It began with how a pock-marked baby was found beside a fence. They knew from the boss the dark story of Paul's birth. Sometimes they would embroider the story in so sharp-witted and intense a fashion that Paul felt as if he were on a red-hot griddle. He was shocked by the cynical details of life which the men described in great detail. Up to then, Paul had neither heard nor known of their existence. When they spoke of his father and mother, humorously describing their appearance and occupation, Paul felt drained, his chest hurt, he choked.

With each repetition of the tour, these feelings would burn more strongly in him. His pock-marked face glowed so that it became terrifying. When the fellows had had enough of this fun they would leave him in peace, forget him. But he who was always silent during the jest, stored up his resentment.

He became more and more taciturn. He frowned so much that a deep, broken wrinkle became fixed on the bridge of his nose. The wrinkle, his silence, bent head, and stern glance earned him the nickname of Little Old Man. He didn't seem to mind and answered willingly to it though he thought of himself as just a boy. Everyone considered him unpleasant and selfish. Finally he was regarded with suspicion as if some unpleasant act were to be expected from him.

Once Nikander remarked that the Little Old Man must have killed a man and was now tormented by the desire to kill another. Or he must be hopelessly in love with the cook, Semenovna. Kolka Shishkin did not agree. It was his opinion that pride was much too developed in the Little Old Man; that periodic thrashings, correctly applied, would cure him. Artiushka ventured to suggest a remedy. He proposed that the Little Old Man's heels be split and short bristles thrown into the open wound. Then he would become so gay he would dance from morn to night.

Grandfather Utkin listened to all this and said:

"You dogs! The boy works. Let him be. What if he doesn't fool around like the rest of you? What's so bad about that? He's a serious boy. That's the kind of character he has."

Then he told a story of a regimental commander who also had a "silent" character and died choking on a fish bone.

By the end of the first week all the workers had a certain, fixed uncomplimentary opinion of Paul. He could not fail to feel this, but he knew he could do nothing to change it. In fact, he thought nothing could help. Everything that he was told to do he did well, willingly and quietly. However, on some rare occasion, when the men in the shop tried out of sheer curiosity to talk to Paul sympathetically, he would answer in one or two words. This left them dissatisfied and they would again fall to teasing, ridicule. This puzzled Paul. Finally, he came to regard every kind word as a trap in which they wished to ensnare him, to place him in a disadvantageous position in order to laugh at him. He was forced to view everything with even greater gloom and suspicion.

So it went on for a month. Paul gradually became accustomed to the idea that he was different from everyone else, since he was treated differently. In the end however, his suspicions were dulled. The shop, too, became used to his silent figure. All the sharp edges were smoothed out, but without improving the situation.

Paul worked, was silent. He was thrashed, beaten, drubbed, kicked, cracked over the head. He became reconciled to these and similar signs of attention. He could not imagine that he could ever expect anything else from this smoky hole and these noisy people.

On Sundays he would go walking, hiding a piece of black bread in his shirt. He found little of interest in the town after he had gone round it three times. After that he limited his walks to Toporkov's neglected garden. There was a wonderful ditch in this garden, behind the bathhouse; the bottom was thick with wild bushy weeds. Paul would go there, lie on his back and look at the sky for hours on end. Around him the wind rustled the burdock, bees buzzed circling the wild gooseberry bushes, some sort of small red insects with black patterns on their backs crawled about. It was here that Paul slowly learned to think.

The shop had almost no meaning for him. It was some sort of senseless puzzle; he had no desire to solve it. Here, in the ditch, life in the shop unfolded before him in a detailed procession—all of it, from Monday morning to Saturday evening. Once, in surveying this panorama, he was struck by one question: Why is all this necessary? Why do we make boots for others and ourselves go barefoot? Why do we drink like Grandfather Utkin? Why do we gamble like Kolka? Why do we "carry on with girls" and then, with bitter humor, complain, as Nikander does every Monday when he tells of some remarkable adventures with "her", or of the fights, of the running away from "him", or from the police? Why do we work and spend our wages on drink, laughing at our own passion for vodka, as the boss does? Why—Why?

Paul thought that if Arefi were well he could have explained all this to him. But Arefi stayed on at the hospital.

Paul had visited the hospital twice. The first time, they simply did not let him in. The second, they

114

said that Arefi would never get well and that there was no need, in fact it would be harmful for Paul to come again. He took this announcement with great surprise. Staring at the doctor, he could not get himself to ask the question he wanted to ask. He turned away and left, depressed.

He decided not to go to see Mikhailo, rightly assuming that nothing pleasant could await him there.

The days passed monotonously, causing Paul no regret and yet not arousing in him a desire to make them different. They merely left him burdened with dull gray thoughts; in time they began to assume an unrealistic character having almost no relation to actual life.

Life goes on as it does, and people live on as they do. Apparently this was the way things had to be. Then it must be good. Sometimes he heard such expressions as "Cursed life!" or "A dog's life!" but these made little impression on him, first, because he heard them most often on the days after the nights before—on Mondays—and second, "a dog's life" to him was not a bad life. Dogs don't have to do anything. They are free and happy, and people often bestow attention, friendship, caresses on them.

In the very beginning, he had tried to understand the workmen and the boss, their behaviour, their intentions. But their attitude toward him entirely-destroyed his interest. He became formal, diffident, automatic. He worked out a pattern of special movements and a mode of life by which he could spend his working day. He began to resemble a little machine, wound up once and for all, which runs on until it either rusts or breaks down.

The others thought him an idiot, and they were right. Indeed there was something idiotic in his unhurried, lethargic movements, in his one-word answers, in his inability to liven up and become interested in the things that engaged everyone around him.

On Sundays, lying in his ditch in the garden, he indulged in fantasy, asking: Why doesn't the sun, wandering along the blue expanse of heaven, get tired of going around like a policeman who always circles the same spot and go off its course? Often Paul thought that if he had his way he would paint the sun another color, or put it into the sky at the same time as the moon—that would be funny!

After two years he was thinner and more dried-up. The pock-marks stood out in greater relief on his face.

During this time, Artiushka left the category of boy-helpers and graduated into that of apprentice. He took the place of red-headed Nikander who had to spend three months in jail for some minor adventure. Kolka was thinking of getting married and opening his own shop. Grandfather Utkin drank and complained of his asthma and his trembling hands which interfered with his work. Observing this, the boss began to drink at home, he made fewer expeditions to the tavern, realizing that the old man was already unable to manage the shop.

Gradually, Paul was initiated into the mysteries of the cobbler's art. Under the despotic guidance of Artiushka, he learned to sole and to tack pieces of leather to the heels of boots. To the surprise of the whole shop, and even the boss himself, he proved to be a rather clever, useful worker. This gave him something of a reputation.

A little while later, Shishkin left the shop. Artiushka's pay was raised, Paul was promoted to his place and a new boy taken on.

Paul was now earning three rubles a month. He stitched to the ceaseless singing of merry Artiushka, to the aged grumbling of Grandfather Utkin, and maintained his usual silence. Since there was not much work, the boss did not hire another craftsman. When the work piled up, he set to himself. This gave him much pleasure and the right to drink even more.

"What a life!" he would often exclaim while pulling the squealing wax thread through the leather.

"You work and drink, and you think its living. A big joke, my boys! Say, isn't it time for dinner? Mishka! Tell Semenovna to set the table and you run to the tavern. Here—take this! Bring half a bottle! Will that be enough, Grandpa?"

Grandpa shook his gray mustache in a contented way, the boss smiled and Mishka, a rogue of ten with curly black hair and quick, darting eyes, ran for the half bottle, cutting a wonderful caper on the way, grimacing gaily to everyone he met.

After ten years of such a life, Paul grew to sizable dimensions and was impressive in appearance. He was tall, a little stooped and very muscular. His rolled up sleeves revealed the brownness of his hands which were covered with blue knotted veins. When he sat bent over his bootmaking, a strong, resilient neck covered with soft fuzz was visible below his chestnut hair. A thick beard was just beginning to break through his pock-marked skin, and his upper lip was already bedecked with a small, light mustache. He did not become more social and lively during this time. He looked out from under his thick, always knitted brows even more suspiciously and gloomy as ever.

In the shop, he continued to be known as the Little Old Man, and had the reputation of being so stupid that he was not in the least tempted by the delights of drinking, nor by visits to various lively places and other such diversions. The workmen were used to him and no longer ridiculed him, partly because they feared his strength, but more because, as they used to say, "nothing can pierce that thick skin."

No one knew what he lived for, since he did none of the things they did. He hardly knew himself. He seemed dull, sedate, capable neither of tears nor of laughter.

The boss, now completely gray, flabby with age, once said of Paul that he had already died and would come alive only when the archangels announced the end of the world. Then, whether he wished or no, he too would have to shake his bones. But, until that time, he would sit unmoved in the shop unless it were destroyed and he were forced to get out of it.

It was evident that Paul wished he could reply. But he contented himself with a pale smile at the boss.

"For this I humbly thank you!" Miron bowed, waiting for something more. Miron was well satisfied with Paul as a worker. Probably he even loved him. He would profess this when drunk. Even when sober he would pay more attention to Paul than to all the others.

There were just two others, Mishka, a swindling, thieving fellow of nineteen, and Goose, a one-eyed man of forty with an incredibly long neck. Goose used to say his neck was long because as a boy he had a remarkable tenor voice and sang in a choir. Now he had no voice at all, unless the heavy screech with which he expressed his thoughts and impressions could be considered a voice.

Artiushka had long since given up the shoemaker's profession. At first he was engaged in petty buying and selling. Then he was a waiter in a tavern. Later he came back to Miron's, stole a pair of newly-made boots, and disappeared. This time he left town.

Old Man Utkin, too, had already gone—on an unlimited vacation. One day he had been stitching away and had sighed deeply. Prior to that, he had been breathing more and more heavily each day. So no one paid any attention, thinking he had a hangover. But this day, he sighed and sighed, and finally, putting down the hammer with which he was beating the leather, he looked up at the ceiling and asked, addressing no one in particular:

"Shall I call the priest, or not?"

Still no one paid any attention because this was an old story. Once before Utkin, apparently thinking that one priest was not enough, had insisted on being taken in a closed carriage to the bishop. This time, after dinner he was so long in leaving his bed behind the stove that they went to wake him. They found he had died.

This made a great impression on Paul. For a long time he stared at everyone with deep, questioning eyes but evidently he could not put into words what was disturbing him and remained silent.

After Utkin was buried Paul began to visit his grave in a deep, dark corner of the cemetery, thick with wild gooseberry and elder bushes that kept the sun off. There, sitting on the ground, Paul looked into the distance through an opening in the stone wall. He saw the hut, the river, the field and the forest. He recalled his own childhood and his silent friend Arefi who had wasted away to death, after two years in the hospital.

Arefi's death did not specially affect Paul; at least there had been no visible expression of grief.

His Sunday walks now extended over a wide area. He no longer went to the ditch in the garden. In adtion to the cemetery, he would go to the mountains beyond the town. From there, the whole town was as clear to him as if it lay in the palm of his hand. He looked at it long. The dull noise of the big, immobile mass rose to him. He saw the tiny black figures that were people shuffle about the streets.

Often he went to the forest. Seeking out a secluded spot, he would lie there for hours, listening to the soft rustle of the trees. Sometimes he would go to nearby villages and wander through the streets, looking at everything intently, searchingly. He would sit in a bar for an hour or two over a bottle of beer or wine, listening to the conversation of the men. Frequently, drunks would attach themselves to him, but his silent, morose figure had such an effect on those only slightly tipsy that they would advise:

"Shoo! Don't touch the man! He's a city man! Beat it!" They would shout to the drunk, then look at Paul suspiciously and belligerently.

He would pay his bill and leave in silence. Once a quiet, warning whisper reached him as he was leaving a bar: "A policeman!" He stopped going to that village.

Dressed in a typical Russian coat, loose trousers, a shirt held by a tufted silk belt, a cap and high boots he had made himself, tall and strong, with a serious face, he little resembled a worker. It would have been difficult to say to what class of society he belonged.

That is the kind of person he was when something happened that "lifted him up and smacked him down", as the boss put it.

"Hey, you, jail-bird!" Miron said one morning to Senka who had just entered the shop. "Clean the samovar to-day. It's dirtier than your mug! And

122

you, Paul, try to finish the lieutenant's boots to-day, you hear?"

"All right," said Paul, adjusting the heel, not looking up at the boss who sat down next to him.

Goose, who now wore glasses, sewed boot-tops on a machine that filled the room with a crisp, sharp clatter.

The May sun shone through the open window into the shop filled with soot, clouds of smoke and the smell of leather; from the street the sound of footsteps and the rumble of carriages filtered in.

Miron looked out the window past which various pairs of human feet flashed. He picked up a piece of leather, inspected it, blinked and said in his elderly, deep voice:

"Interesting lodgers have come to live with us. Two. They're gay girls. Watch your step, boys!"

No one commented on this announcement. Undisturbed, he continued after a pause:

"Now, you, Paul, should get acquainted with them. At least you might learn how to talk. Why, you're like a monk. Or are you planning to go to Heaven? Don't overwork yourself, my boy! They don't allow shoemakers in. They have no use for them, everybody goes barefoot up there. The weather is too heavenly there. Yes, yes!"

"De-li-ci-ous ice-c-r-eam!" a high voice shouted on the street.

"So go ahead, start a delicate relationship with the lodgers, Paul! Eh? They'll make you red-hot, melt you, and mold you into a new human being. Solomon says: 'Surrender not your strength to women, nor direct your way to the destroyers of kings', but that's not written for us. These women are merry things. Yes, sir! Give the women freedom and they'll turn God's world upside down. Oh, what a ball they would stage! First of all, all the married women would leave their husbands. And the girls—they'd march the men off one-two-three to the altar! That would be a glorious mess!"

Miron was in great form that day. Not pausing for a moment, he spun a great tale, as the pious Goose characterized his fantasy. The latter finished his work on the sewing machine and examined the boot-top, thoughtfully, attempting to render the majestic "Heavenly Father" in a falsetto voice. A snake's hissing came out, instead of a song, and Goose, rubbing his long neck, coughed energetically, spat to one side, then to the other.

"Why so red, Paul?" Miron asked, suddenly noticing his worker. "Your forehead's all of a sweat!"

"I don't know!" Paul answered dully, wiping

his forehead with his hand, smearing it black.

"Now, don't you go smearing yourself with ashes. It won't help!" the boss remarked in a resounding tone. "Your eyes are muddy. Aren't you well?"

"Yes. Not well.... I can't...."

"Well, why are you sitting there?" the boss asked. "Chuck your work. Someone else can finish stitching the boots. Go ahead and lie down. Rest up."

Paul rose, and swaying drunkenly, went to the door.

"I'll lie down in the cellar, so that if something...." but he left without completing the sentence.

Walking through the yard, his legs were shaky. His head felt heavy, whirled; red and green circles floated in front of his eyes.

The air in the cellar was damp and heavy. It seemed saturated with thick steam. Paul unbuttoned his shirt at the neck, threw off the heavy apron sewn from old flour sacks. Then he lay down on a sack of hay on some damp boards, with his arms supporting his neck.

It was dark in the cellar. The rays of the sun filtered through the cracks in the door, cutting the darkness into thin, shimmering ribbons which appeared and disappeared. He heard steps overhead. His head hummed strangely. The beating at his temples intoxicated him, the blood boiled quickly and strongly in his veins. Breathing came hard. He smelled damp, hot blood.

The red and green spots leaped before his eyes, sometimes small and glistening like the eyes of a cat, then large and dark, like pieces of morocco, falling from somewhere above, twirling about in mid air, lightly, like dry autumn leaves.

Paul lay, his eyes wide open, and tried not to move. He was afraid that if he did move he would drop into a deep abyss, float there in hot, suffocating steam. Over and around him, everything whirled, tottered. There was a monotonous high ringing in his ears.

So passed several curiously slow minutes. Then, suddenly, sunlight streamed through an open door; the familiar voice of Senka rang out sharply:

"Coming to dinner, Paul?"

"I don't want any dinner," Paul answered. It seemed strange that it was only dinner time. His own voice seemed even stranger. How could it sound so dull, steady, so much as usual? It was such a long time since he had left the shop.

Again it was dark in the cellar. The light had jumped right out of it. Once again the slow minutes dragged. His ears were filled with a sickening sound. It seemed to Paul that something humid and hot was sucking him into itself. He fell into a stupor in which he felt thirst and gasped harder for air . . .

"Some dummy is lying here."

"Probably the shoemaker from the basement. Drunk."

"Well, let him be."

Paul opened his eyes and weakly turned his head toward the door.

It was now light in the cellar. Two women stood at the door. One was lifting the door leading into the cellar, while the other stood near her, a pitcher of milk in one hand and a package in the other. Her large blue eyes peered into the corner where Paul lay while she talked to her friend in a clear, rich, throaty voice:

"Well, make it snappy, Katerina!"

"Don't rush me! You try lifting it yourself!" Katerina retorted, pushing at the damp, heavy door. Her voice was dull, coarse.

"Just see how the shoemaker is staring at me! Oh!" the first girl continued. "As if he wants to eat me up."

"Douse him with milk!"

"I can't spare the milk."

Paul stared at them with shining feverish eyes. They both seemed to float in the fog far from him, so far that when he hoarsely begged, "Give me something to drink" he did not expect them to hear.

But they had heard. The one with the blue eyes and the pitcher of milk threw her package on the floor and came to the corner, holding her skirt with her free hand. The other, standing half-way up the steps leading to the cellar, watched her with interest.

"A hangover is no fun, Katya. Throw me a handful of snow. I don't want to waste milk on him."

Paul heard this and said again, hoarsely:

"Hurry. A drink. . . ."

Then he saw the blue eyes over him, staring into his face. "Katya, he's so pock marked! Ooooh! Why, he's not drunk! Can't smell liquor. Katya, this man's sick, honest to God, he's sick! He's all hot and he breathes like a steam engine! Oh, those damn devils up there! They've dragged a sick man into the cellar, the swine! Drink, here, drink! How long have you been lying here? Eh? Don't you have a family? Why haven't they taken you to a hospital?"

Squatting down near Paul, she held the jug to his mouth. He clung with trembling hands, thirstily gulping the milk. She showered him with questions, apparently forgetting that he could not possibly speak and drink at the same time.

"Thank you!" he said finally, pushing the jug away. His head dropped back on the sack.

"Who dragged you into this cold place? Was it

the boss? It's easy to see he's a dog!" she said indignantly, and touched his forehead with her hand.

"I, myself . . . ." Paul began, not taking his eyes from her.

"Smart! Very clever! Have you been like this long?"

"Just to-day. . . ."

"Mmmm! Probably been fighting it for a week and it finally laid you out. Oh, oh, oh! What shall we do now? Katerina! What shall we do with him?"

"What do you think? Put him on ice? Or maybe you want to take him to your place? Suppose he croaks? You fool! Go on, go on!"

Paul turned his head with great difficulty and looked at the other woman, still standing on the cellar steps. Her glance was coldly curious. Her jeering words made him feel worse. Sighing, he turned his eyes to the one near him.

She did not answer her friend. She frowned, then her face cleared.

"You lie here!" she said in decision, bending right down to Paul's face. "You lie here. I'll be right back with vinegar and vodka with pepper. Do you hear?"

And she rose quickly and disappeared.

Both women left, leaving the door open. The sound of an explosive argument between them reached Paul.

He might have thought that everything that had just happened was only delirium. But the soft taste of milk was still in his mouth, he felt the wet milk that had poured on his shirt. And his face still held the sensation of a soft hand, gently caressing his cheeks and forehead. He waited for her return. He was overcome with a strange curiosity which crowded out all the sick feeling. He wanted terribly to know what would happen next. Never before had he had such a strong desire to know what lay ahead. Turning on his side, his back to the door, he fixed his inflamed, sick eyes on the courtyard.

She soon returned, carrying in one hand a bottle, the neck of which was covered by a cup, and in the other, a wet rag.

"Here, now, drink," she said, but when Paul stretched his hand out for the cup she poured the stuff directly into his wide open mouth. As the liquid went down, it set his whole mouth and throat on fire and made him cough.

"It works good," she exclaimed in triumph and immediately plastered the cold, wet rag soaked in vinegar on his forehead. Obediently and silently, Paul let her do all this, his eyes fixed on her all the time.

"Well, now, we can talk. Your boss is a stingy guy. The hell with him! I, myself, will take you to the hospital to-morrow. You're feeling pretty bad, aren't you? Well, you'll have to wait—you'll soon feel a little better. It's hard for you to talk, isn't it?"

"No. It's all right. I can talk."

"No, no. You keep quiet. Doctors always order sick people not to talk. You lie quiet. Rest."

Evidently finding nothing else to talk about, she looked about her with the expression of a person who suddenly feels sick at heart.

Paul continued to stare at her and thought, why is she doing all this for me? I'm a stranger to her. She must be that lodger the boss spoke about. What did he call her? He had to know.

"What—is—your—name?" he whispered softly.

"Me? Natalya Krivtsova. Why?"

"Just so."

"Oh!" she said indefinitely and, having looked him over from head to foot, she hummed softly to herself.

"And you?" she suddenly asked, interrupting her singing.

"Paul."

"How old are you?"

"Twenty."

"That means you'll soon go into the army!" she concluded and was quiet again. After a pause, "Don't you have any relatives?"

"No. I'm a foundling," Paul said quietly. His head began to ache terribly again. The thirst came back.

"O-o-o-h!" She moved closer. Her blue eyes inspected him in amazement, as if she could not understand how such a big, substantial person could be a foundling.

"Another drink!"

"Here, here, right away!" she replied, bustling about. Filling the cup with milk, she quickly put her hand under his head, lifted him and whispered:

"Good health! Christ be with you!"

He drank. Between swallows, he looked at her face which earlier had been almost carefree, but now was thoughtful and sad. This expression was more familiar and understandable to Paul. It encouraged him to speak to her.

As soon as he had finished the milk, he said suddenly and loudly: "Tell me, why are you doing this?"

"What am I doing?" She looked puzzled and stared at Paul in question.

"Why, for me . . . all this. How much you've given me . . . taking care of me . . . and everything. Why?" Paul blurted out, then became frightened seeing that she moved away as if hurt.

"I don't know why. Just so! You're a human

being, aren't you? Or aren't you? You're a funny one, really!'' and she shrugged her shoulders.

Paul shook his head in an indefinite way. Turning to the wall, he was quiet. Strange thoughts wandered about in his sick head. For the first time in his life someone had been kind to him. And who? One of those women he disliked and feared, remembering Ārefi's attitude toward them. One of those they talked about in the shop. For some time, he had been secretly thinking a great deal about women, concealing these thoughts even from himself, indignant with himself because of such thoughts. Woman— she is the eternal enemy of man, an enemy who waits only for some convenient moment to enslave him and suck out his blood. This was the opinion he heard more often than any other. Sometimes, meeting a beautiful girl, timidly and hurriedly running up the street, Paul would look at her and think: how can she be an enemy when she is such a little chick. His fearful curiosity, which he could not help showing when others spoke about women, made him the butt of much ridicule from the boss and the workers in the shop. Often, they would assume false attitudes of repentance for their passion and praise Paul for his purity. He understood, in a general way, that woman plays a tremendous and all-embracing role in life, but he could in no way make a connection between this deduction, arrived at through his own thinking and feeling, with another deduction, the accepted one, that woman was an enemy.

Once the boss had lectured him. "Watch out for women, Paul. Don't give in to a woman. Then you'll get on. Anyone you ask will tell you that there is no heavier chain in the world than a woman. They're greedy animals. They like to live well and work little. Believe me, I've lived fifty two years in this world and been married twice."

Yet here she was, terrible, mysterious woman. The first to bring him a pleasant consciousness that he, morose and different from everyone else, that he, Paul, was worthy of her care. She came to him, sat by him, he who was alone in the world, with no one he could call friend.

"What is she doing now?" Paul thought, and turned very quietly so he could see her.

She sat on the floor and thoughtfully looked into the court yard through the half-open door. Her face was very kind and beautiful, soft; her blue eyes gracious, her lips crimson and full.

"Thank you for being so kind," Paul said quietly, stretching his hand out to her in an involuntary gesture.

She shivered, glanced askance at him, but did not take his hand.

"I thought you had fallen asleep. Look here, you've got to get out of here. You've got to get out of here at once. It's too damp here. Come on now, get up!"

Paul did not withdraw his hand and repeated insistently:

"Thank you for being so kind!"

"Good heavens! There you go again! Well, what about it? What kindness? It's hot outside, so I'm glad to sit here for a while. Come on now, get up!"

She seemed irritated. Helping him to rise, she turned her head away, as if not wishing to meet his eyes.

Paul rose, the blood rushed to his head. He heard the dull noises again.

"It's hard for me . . ." he whispered, his legs shaking. He felt as though the pain was breaking his bones.

"That's all right. Somehow you've got to stand it! You can't stay here." Supported by her, he floated in a sort of fog through the court yard. Through the fog he saw the sly smiles on the faces of the boss and Goose, standing on the threshold of the shop.

"I can't go . . . further!" he said hoarsely, as he felt himself slip into a bottomless pit.

6

For the first time in his life Paul became aware that a hospital was more than a building. Sickening yellow walls, the foul smell of medications, exhausted and irritable orderlies, the disinterested faces of doctors and their assistants, moans, delirium, the whims of the sick, gray dressing-gowns, night-caps, the shuffle of slippers dragging on the stone floor—all these fused into a gray pattern of despondency, lifelessness, the heavy, incessant, gnawing of grief . . .

Paul was delirious for eleven days. It was now the

fifth day since the crisis had passed. He had begun to get well. The attendant had told him that the boss had come once, Goose, twice, "your sister" twice, once with a friend and once alone. She had left some tea, sugar, jam, and other little things in a bag.

When the orderly mentioned his sister Paul's jaw dropped in surprise. But then he realized that he meant Natalya. For some reason, that made Paul happy.

"What a girl!" he whispered. How pleasant it would be to see her.

But typhus cases were not permitted to have visitors. Not until he was transferred to Ward 5 would visitors be allowed.

"No one but doctors and orderlies can enter here," the orderly explained. Although this was announced with some sense of sad pride in the special privilege, Paul had only one question: How soon could he be transferred to Ward 5?

He was told it depended on the nose. "Now your nose is yellow and dry, but soon it will swell and get red. When that happens, you'll be transferred. Typhus cases are always transferred according to the nose. That's the way we do things. This is the seventh year that we've been fooling around with that sort of thing. That's our routine."

The orderly was a great one for talk. Since, of the

nine patients, Paul was the only one capable of listening, and understanding—the others being in no condition to engage in conversation—he had to bear the burden of this gentleman all by himself. The orderly was a small, bony, red-headed fellow with melancholy gray eyes. In his free time he sat on Paul's cot and rambled.

"Getting better? I see, I see that everything is going all right. Ward 5 for you soon. It's a good thing that you are sick. Typhus is a remarkable sickness—it purifies. A man could have been the worst scoundrel, with a soul impregnated through and through with sinful filth. But once he gets sick with typhus —he is purified! That's because of the delirium. You know, in delirium your soul leaves your body and travels around and suffers—and repents. Oh, yes! I suppose you'll say that many people die of typhus, but that's all right, too. That's man's fate. The Bible says so. You know, people don't die of typhus itself. The material wears out—gets rubbed out from living, and the soul needs a new suit, that is, a new apartment. And for man there's only one apartment —the earth. Oh, yes! Have any of your relatives died? No? Ah! Eleven have died in my family. One of them was even taken alive by the earth. He was a plumber. He was laying a pipe, and the earth went —bang! and no more Nikolai. The earth just swallowed him. They dug him out, but he was a goner! Oh, yes! The earth will always get you. You can't get around it. You can't run away. Why, even if you jump into the river you find yourself in the ground. Jump into the fire—you still become dirt. The earth looks out for itself. She'll soon be calling me. Anasim, my friend, she'll say, come on, please, into the grave! And I'll have to lie there. No matter what you do, you must go, and that's that. That's the way it is, my boy. You can kick up a fuss; I don't want to go, you say. But she breathes on your heart, you keel over, and you're through. You're done for. Nothing left. The world is alive only so long as you walk around in it."

Sometimes he talked for two hours at a stretch. He was not concerned whether people listened to him or not. He spoke his gloomy speeches until his staring eyes became glazed and acquired a strange, dim hue, as if a filmy cloud covered his pupils. Then his speech would become muffled, more disjointed, his sentences shorter. Finally he would sigh deeply and cut himself off in the middle of a word. Cold terror stared out of his eyes.

The orderly's conversation made hardly any impression on Paul, who almost never listened. He was sunk in his own thoughts, now brightened by a hope, a feeling that the future had something in store for

140

him. What it was, he could not clearly imagine. He had little enough material with which to build castles in the air. He knew about life only from the words of others. Up to this time he had been able to avoid active participation in it. But now he felt that something new, big, unknown, was approaching, that it would create a new kind of life for him. In the strict sense of the word, he had almost never been able to think cogently. He did not possess enough words, his ideas were too meagre. But ever since he had regained consciousness in the hospital and remembered the glance in Natalya's blue eyes there was a new awareness in him, many new sensations had been born in his dark soul. The orderly's news that she had been to the hospital twice, heightened this feeling even more.

For twenty years no one had paid any attention to him. But he was a human being; he could not live without attention. He was also somewhat exceptional in that he was entirely alone, and therefore had craved attention with a greater thirst than others. This desire was entirely instinctive, unconscious. Paul had had no idea what this attention would be like, nor where it would appear, nor in what form. And now it had come. It had come, and he sincerely hoped that this was only the beginning, that the future held for him a whole world of new feelings. With each successive day, the purely animal sensation of regaining his physical strength so shattered by illness, kindled in him an even greater desire for the quickest possible realization of the future.

Anasim, the orderly, was very sad when Paul was transferred to Ward 5. He had lost his only listener. He insisted that Paul was being removed prematurely; he might die yet, the nose had not yet swelled sufficiently.

One day, when Paul, sunk in his muddled half-thoughts, half-sensations, lay on his cot watching the flies travel along the ceiling, a soft voice just above his head said:

"Paul!"

He shuddered, frightened. This was so unexpected. She, too, was somewhat embarrassed.

"Hello. Thank heaven, you've been transferred! Here, I brought . . ." and she pushed a little bag into his hands.

Flushed, frightened, she looked around the ward with caution.

Paul's fear disappeared in the intense joy which reddened his cheeks faintly.

"Thank you humbly! I most humbly thank you! I'm very grateful to you. Very! Please sit down right here, or right here. . . . No, right here it would be comfortable. Thank you. You're so good. Please

142

be assured of that . . ." he stammered, his eyes glowing. He was completely transformed.

She was even more embarrassed at this unexpected reception. She continued to look all around, first at one patient, then at another, as if fearful that she would find one who would be unpleasant to her.

"All right. I'll sit down. Don't trouble yourself. It's bad for you . . ." she whispered, continuing her search.

Paul, enthusiastic, reassured her.

"Don't you worry. These are all good, sick people . . . we talk . . . they're decent. They mean no harm . . . they're very pleasant people. Oh, how happy I am that you're here!" he concluded almost in a shout.

She had completed her inspection of the ward and sighing, smiled a wide kind smile.

"I'm glad you're getting better. I've been here before, you know. You were unconscious. Don't upset yourself, please. I brought you . . . the doctor permitted me to . . . Eat it!" and she began to untie the bag.

But Paul, overcome with happiness, seized the bag with trembling hands, and said:

"Believe me, you're just an angel from heaven to me, as God is my witness! . . ."

"What are you saying?" and again she was embarrassed.

"No, it's so. I don't know how to say it. I don't know how. I'm always silent. But I do understand, you know. Permit me to tell you that. After all, what are you to me? A stranger. And I'm a stranger, too. But, you see, you're the first person to come . . . And then down in the cellar . . . There was no reason for you to do it. Why, I'm all alone, and I've never known a kind thing in all my life. . . . That's the whole point. Do you understand? This is very, very good! Wonderful!" and he shook her hands excitedly.

"Calm yourself. This is very bad, you know, to carry on like that. They may not let me in anymore . . ." she tried to quiet him, still embarrassed by his impulsive, disconnected speech. But she understood very well that it was she who was the cause of his happy excitement.

"They won't let you in?" he exclaimed in fright, peering into her face. He protested: "That's impossible! You're like a sister! They can't do that! Who told you? That's just nonsense. I have rights . . . I'll complain . . ."

"Oh, you're a funny fellow. Complain about what? I didn't mean it. What are you going to do, start a revolution here? You're very funny!"

Actually he now seemed a little ridiculous to her in his ecstasy. She could not quite understand why he should be so excited. But she found it flattering and pleasant to know that she was the cause of it. She became a little bolder and began to display a little despotism, to which he submitted completely. It was as pleasant to him to submit as it was to her to demand. She forced him to eat a roll, adjusted his pillow, asked him how he felt, and finally spoke to him sternly He melted completely under her care and attention; she was amused.

He was now quiet, content merely to regard her face with happy, surprised eyes. She told him that soon he would be out, he could visit her, have tea with her, walk in the forest with her, go boat riding —she drew wonderful pictures for him.

Before he realized it, the visiting hours had passed and she had to leave.

At parting, Paul looked pitifully into her eyes and begged in a soft whisper that she come again.

Alone, he closed his eyes and immediately saw her; small, plump, fair, with rosy cheeks, piquant, sharply-upturned nose, her large caressing eyes. She was so beautiful and so fresh! Her dark blouse and skirt, her smoothly combed and braided hair—all this made her very simple, dear and kind. When she spoke, her small, pretty, shining teeth flashed between her full lips Above all, kindness radiated from her.

Paul kept thinking of this image of her and felt himself changed. He was surprised that he could speak with her so quickly and so easily. And she was so good, so dear to him. Filled with tender emotions, he fell asleep.

The next day passed in a happy fog. He continued to picture what had happened the day before. He smiled and whispered a thousand times, "thank you most humbly!" Through this one phrase, repeated, he expressed a multitude of different emotions.

To-morrow was another visiting day; possibly she would come. He imagined how it would be, kept making up sentences with which to praise her. . . . He also imagined he was already well, boating along the river with her, telling her about Arefi.

To-morrow came. His whole body trembling feverishly, he looked hungrily at the door from morning until evening. He waited, expecting her to appear at any moment and begin searching among the sick as she had done the first time. Then she would sit by his cot and they would talk. . . . But the day passed and she did not come.

That night, Paul could not fall asleep for a long time. He tried to imagine what could have prevented her from coming. In the morning he awoke with a splitting headache. He was lethargic, apathetic.

The next day he lay silent, not moving, thinking of nothing, imagining nothing, expecting nothing. Many more visiting days came and went and still she did not come.

Paul lay in his bed and tried to recall all the bad things he had heard about women. He forced himself to ascribe these to his new acquaintance. But, somehow, nothing bad would stick to her. He tried to imagine her dirty, drunk, a thief, swearing at him, ridiculing him. Nevertheless she remained in the end simple, beautiful, and kind.

The days flowed on. He was already taking walks along the corridor whose windows faced the street. He would stop at one of the windows and think of his release—feeling an overwhelming desire to walk on the sun-flooded streets among all those healthy, bustling, busy people.

Every woman walking toward the hospital roused in him a faint tremor of hope. For half an hour he would stare at the end of the corridor to see whether she would appear. But she did not come; Paul felt cheated, sad.

One day he heard the orderly's voice:

"Paul Gibly, wanted in the office."

He rushed there quickly.

"Here, take it! They brought it for you," a thin, tall doctor's assistant said, twirling his mustaches. He handed Paul a package wrapped in paper.

"And—who brought it?" Paul asked, taking it with trembling hands.

"An old man who said . . ."

Paul shook his head sadly. He put the package down before the assistant.

". . . that he's your boss? There was a woman with him, with a bandage around her face. She was young."

Paul trembled and picked up the package again.

"Was she very much bandaged?" he asked.

The assistant's brows and mustaches rose high.

"How do you mean, was she very much bandaged?"

"No, I—nothing. I humbly thank you. She must have had a toothache."

"Hmm?" the assistant shook his head. "It's possible she had a toothache. Well?"

"She said nothing about me?" Paul asked softly, anxiously.

"Yes, she did. 'He,' she said, 'is something of a fool, so excuse him.' You can go. You're excused."

Paul turned and left. He understood he was being laughed at. Now he thought he knew why she had not come to see him all this time. She simply had a toothache, but as soon as she felt better she had come. What a kind person she was!

A week later he stood once again in the office before the doctor's assistant who was poring over some book and was clicking away on an abacus.

"Did you get all your things?" he asked, and not waiting for Paul's answer, added: "Very well. Go. Good day!"

Paul bowed and went out into the street. Half an hour later, drunk with sunlight and exertion, his eyes befogged, his head whirling, he entered the shop. He was met by the boss.

"Ah! You've come! Good boy! Hello! You sure got thin. Well, that's all right, at least you've learned to smile."

Paul had actually smiled as he looked around the shop. He was filled with good, tender feelings when he opened the door of the shop and stood on the threshold. Everything was so nice here, so familiar, so close. Even the white spots on these sooty old walls—heaven only knows how they happened to remain untouched by the black layers of soot—seemed to smile at him. And there was his bed in the corner, two pictures hanging over it—The Day of Judgment and The Road to Life.

Mishka stood open-mouthed, his lively, excited black eyes fixed on Paul, an expression of the most active pleasure on his face. And the boss, too, seemed glad that he had come.

Miron Toporkov continued:

"Well, well, come in and sit down, rest. You must be tired. Mishka and I have been taking care of everything. Goose took to drinking. I didn't want to take on anyone else. I kept thinking you'd come any minute. Well, that's good. Now we'll get to stitching. We'll make things hum, and how! I've been working again. I haven't been drinking for a long time—I drink, of course, but I don't drink enough to get tipsy."

Paul listened and was more and more pleased, both because the boss spoke so gaily and because there was in his tone something intimate, something good. Paul felt warm and soft inside.

"Now, Miron, we'll really get to work!" Paul said with animation and assurance, when the boss had finished talking and had turned to measuring a piece of leather over a hole in an old boot-top. "I humbly thank you for having visited me. It was important to me," Paul added warmly, "because I'm all alone in this world . . ."

"Whee!" the boss whistled, interrupting. "So that's how you're talking now! Ech, boy! I tell you, there's no bad without good. Before your illness you would sooner have burst than say such words. That's good. Time! High time! And another thing. I'll tell you what. You go to this Natalya. Go on. Though she's that kind, still you ought to thank her. You have no idea how she worried about you! She's really got it bad. Almost every day she'd drop by and say, 'Have you been there? Did you go? Have you seen?' . . . Yes, brother, she's still got some good in her. She's only human and that can't be held against her. Go on, then. Go to her! Imagine! A girl like that— and suddenly! Oh, what pretty speeches she made the last time we drank to your health! So help me, I've never heard the like of it in my life! 'How do they look at the like of us?' she says to me. 'We're swine, filthy dogs. Isn't it so?' 'True,' says I. 'And he,' says she,—that is, you, she means—'met me like one of his very own. That's what! You understand, grandfather Miron?' 'I understand,' says I. 'Well,' says she, 'I must pay him back for it with the same kind of treatment.' Seems simple, doesn't it? But it's strange, at the same time. Not at all like in real life. Not the way things really happen. It doesn't match things as we really know them . . ."

Beyond that Miron could not progress. He had stumbled on some obstacle not visible to Paul who listened with an expression of the deepest attention and quiet happiness on his pock-marked face. He continued to look at the boss even when the latter, finally convinced of the impossibility of formulating his thoughts, waved his hand broadly and was silent.

Paul was silent too. What Miron had said pleased him so much that he felt compelled to express something of what filled his heart and possessed his mind. But, unable to do so, he began again to thank his boss.

"I'm deeply grateful to you, boss, for all your words. So thankful!" And he stretched out his hand, not able to say precisely how grateful he was. "This illness turned out to my advantage. You put it correctly. I was like an animal before I was sick. But now I see that I am a man. People care about me. Most hu-u-mbly I thank you! . . ." He was short of breath in his intense desire to open his heart to his boss.

"Now, that's nonsense! What if you weren't a treat before your illness? You were a clumsy guy, that's true. But I must tell you that I'm not quite sure which way is better—to keep your distance, or be friends with people. They're very seldom good company . . . and you don't often have a good time with them . . . well, you can, but you have to keep your mouth shut, and your fists handy. And there's no use being angry if they cheat you, because everyone wants to. Life is so crowded that it's impossible not to push the guy next to you. But don't take it.

It's better to kick than to be kicked. But above all, watch out for women! They're so sly that you won't even notice how they sting you. One, a woman smiles at you. Two, she kisses you. Three, she praises you. Four, you're working for her. Five—you're fed up. You ask to be free, but oh, dear, oh, dear! These cats have such claws that you can't get away! You die about five times before your death, my friend! . . ."

Miron was inspired and, without interrupting his work, philosophized till the evening.

Paul sat opposite him and listened attentively, picking at something with an awl. But attention to his boss's monologue did not crowd out certain persistent thoughts that had been stored up in his head.

"Enough!" Miron said, ending his philosophizing and his work at the same time. "Lie down, and rest. Or—why don't you go out into the street and get some air?"

"No, I'd better go see her . . ." Paul said meekly, with downcast eyes.

"You mean Natalya? Hmm . . . Well, go ahead," said the boss, thoughtfully.

But when Paul walked out of the shop, he shouted:

"Look out, now, that she doesn't marry you! Hee, hee! You never notice how it happens . . . They're skillful! . . ."

This remark displeased Paul. He felt he knew—she was not at all like the others. He himself had tried to think the worst of her, but it simply would not stick. She was kind. That was all there was to it!

Preoccupied with these conflicting thoughts, Paul without noticing how he got up the stairs, found himself in the attic before the small door which was not quite closed. He felt ill at ease. He was about to go in, but hesitated; he should cough first to announce himself. But although his cough was loud, it aroused no sign of life behind the door.

"Probably sleeping," he thought, but did not leave. His hands behind his back, he continued to stand there, secretly hoping that at any moment she would awake.

A dull noise reached him from the street. The sun beating down on the roof during the day had made the attic stuffy. A smell like that of overheated earth tickled his nostrils.

Suddenly he noticed the door opening slowly. He stepped back, respectfully removed his cap, bowed low, and not lifting his head, waited for her to say something. But she said nothing. Then he lifted his head and gasped. No one stood before him; no one was in the room. The door had apparently been opened by the wind blowing through the window.

He glanced into the room. Things were thrown about in it. The room had not been cleaned. The bed near the wall was rumpled; in front of it on a table there were dirty dishes, pieces of food, cigarette butts, two beer bottles, a samovar, cups. A red skirt, shoes, crumpled paper flowers were strewn about on the floor.

The sight saddened Paul. He wanted to leave, but instead, prompted by an inner impulse, stepped over the threshold. It was a wretched hole with a ceiling like the cover of a coffin, papered with cheap blue wall-paper. The paper was torn in spots and hung loosely from the wall. This, together with the general disorder, gave the room a strange appearance, as if it had been turned inside out.

Paul sighed deeply, walked up to the window, and sat down on the chair.

"Why don't I go?" he thought, and knew he had no desire to leave the place. "How can I go? She isn't here, the apartment isn't locked and everything is thrown about. . . . She can't be far away . . here somewhere . . ."

And he looked out the window hoping to see her.

The town looked strange from the window. Actually, there was no town, only roofs, and among them green islands of gardens. Green, red, brown roofs, each clinging to the other in a haphazard, disorderly way. From among them, the steeple of a church crowned by a cross, faintly lit by the last rays of the setting sun, rose up into the sky. On the outskirts of the town the thin smoke of evening mist rose and softly floated over the roofs, making them softer, darker. The spots of greenery fused with the houses. Paul saw the evening enveloping the earth with its shadows. He felt pleasantly sad. Off in the distance, beyond the town, where the sky was darker, two stars appeared, one large and reddish, cheery and bright, the other, just peeping out and trembling as if in fright, appearing and disappearing.

It would be good to be the sort of man who could understand the order of things, all this—the evening, the sky, the stars, the sleeping town and his own thoughts; a man who knows the whys and the wherefores, what thought and meaning is hidden in the order of the universe; a man who understood the world would also know why he exists, and what his place in life is. Such a man could perhaps make all life as soft and warm as this evening and unite people so that each man would see himself in another man and not be afraid.

Carried away by his thoughts, Paul sat at the window, unaware of the passing of time, although it was becoming darker before his very eyes. Only when he heard someone shout in the courtyard and looked down did he become conscious that he had been sitting there long. It was completely dark and the entire sky was studded with stars. He was sleepy; he sighed and went toward the door. As he left the room, he heard heavy, uneven steps and paused.

A bobbing figure was swaying up the steps. It was whimpering, almost crying. Paul stepped aside, stood behind the door.

"The lousy crooks!" a drunken voice mumbled.

Paul thought it was someone come to see Natalya. He was dumbfounded when he realized that it was she herself. Even at that distance he could smell the vodka on her; when she came near he saw that she was dishevelled, rumpled, could barely talk. He felt pity for her, but for some reason did not step out to help her. He remained behind the door. She shoved the door with her shoulder, pressing Paul to the wall, and entered the room. Immediately there was a crash of falling glasses and bottles.

"Go to the devil . . . everybody . . . to hell with . . . it . . ."

Paul sensed a hurt, bitter tone in the drunken voice. He did not move. He held his breath and listened although it was not pleasant for him to do so. Then there was sobbing and shouts of protests.

"He beat me up . . . the dog! Why did he beat me? I could have demanded . . . my money! I could have

. . . the swindler! Three rubles . . . I need them. A-a-nd you thought, well, she's . . . that kind, you can beat her . . . you can beat her! No, you lie! . . . lie! . . . lie! I can feel too. Well, all right, I'm no human being . . . Well, all right . . . not a human being . . . but that kind . . . but, but haven't I a right to . . . my . . . it's my full right . . . to demand . . . three rubles!"

She hissed "three rubles" so penetratingly and with such drunken spitefulness and grief that Paul was himself filled with bitter grief and spite against someone, and quickly ran downstairs. On the last step he heard the noise of things falling, dishes breaking.

"That must be the table . . ." he said loudly, already standing in the courtyard. He did not know what to do. He felt he ought to do something. Standing there, cap in hand, he listened to his pounding heart, felt as if his chest were in a vise . . . Everything was confused; he did not have one clear thought.

"Bastards!" His voice was low. He remembered every swear word he had ever heard and repeated all of them in furious whispers. Later, when he felt better, he walked through the gate and sat on the bench, his back pressed hard against the wall.

He had a continuous vision of female figures walking along dark, deserted streets, muttering spitefully . . . A gnawing grief grew stronger within him. He rose and went back to the shop.

"Well, Paul, how's everything?" the boss asked next morning. He smiled slyly, seeing him. "Were you there? Did you thank her, eh?"

"She . . . wasn't . . . home," Paul answered sullenly, avoiding the boss's eyes.

"Yeah? Well, let it be so. We'll write it down that she wasn't, so to speak, at home!" and he sat down to work opposite Paul.

"The girl sure gets around," the boss again. "Too bad. Such a good-hearted girl, too. Really too bad! Well, all you can do is have pity. Can't do more about it. It's one of those things."

Paul was silent, feverishly jerking the waxed thread through the leather. The boss sang through his nose.

"Miron," Paul said, turning to his boss after a prolonged silence.

"Yes?" the boss asked, lifting his head.

"Do you think she could get out of this rut?"

"She? Hmm! Maybe. But it's more likely she won't. But on the other hand she might. It's hard to say, my friend. Oh, yes! Of course, if there'd be a fellow, an iron man, who'd grab her in his strong hands . . . Well—even then it'd still be a matter of argument who'd come out on top. But the thing is,

159

nowadays there are no more fools, because there are as many brides as flies in summertime. Even good brides don't get a good price. Take Goose, for instance. He got married, got two hundred rubles with her, and the girl has an angel's face and she can read. Of course, she'll cheat him because—what kind of a bargain is he? He's close to fifty and she's only seventeen. But a girl like that married Goose, and even gave him two hundred rubles—just so he'd take her! There are a lot of brides nowadays. They come cheap. And why? Too crowded to live, my boy. Heaps of people are born. Now, if they'd forbid people from getting married, say, for about five years— that would be another matter. That would be smart! Really it would, as God is my witness! Eh?" and, carried away by his own idea, old man Miron began to develop his theory in detail.

Paul was silent. One would have said that he was listening attentively. But at the moment when Miron had finally succeeded in solving the problem of artificially decreasing the population, Paul interrupted:

"Miron, what if I were to give her a present?"

"Her? You mean Natalya?" the boss asked, after a long silence. He stared at the ceiling, somewhat hurt that Paul had cut short his fantastic effusion.

"You can give her a present. Why not? She's spent money on you, you know."

And again he was silent. Then he began to hum.

After dinner they sat opposite each other, energetically working some leather. The day was hot. Despite the open door and window it was stuffy in the shop. The boss wiped the sweat from his forehead, swore at the heat, thought of Hell where the temperature was no doubt ten degrees lower. He would gladly have gone there had he not promised to get these cursed boots done.

Paul, his forehead wrinkled, lips tightly pressed, was bent over his sewing.

"So you say, she's a good girl, after all?" he suddenly asked.

"So that's what's on your mind! Well, yes, she's all right. So what?" The boss looked searchingly at Paul's bent head.

"Nothing!" he answered shortly.

"That's not saying very much!" the boss laughed.

"What can I say?" Paul sounded sad, perplexed, tired, weak.

Again they were quiet.

"So she can't change? So there's nothing to be done?" The questions were timid. Miron did not answer.

Paul waited a little longer and suddenly protested:

"Well, that's wrong! It's not right! She's good, and yet she's doomed: That's a damn shame!" He kicked the table.

"Whee!" the boss whistled through his teeth, then laughed sarcastically. "Oh, you're a greenhorn, Paul. You're like a sheep led to slaughter. Ha, ha, ha!"

In the evening after work, Paul went into the hall of the shop. Standing at the door leading into the courtyard he looked up at the window of the attic. There was a light, but no movement. He stood there for a long time and waited to see whether her figure would appear. Then he could wait no longer; he went out into the street and sat again on the bench where he had sat the night before.

He could not get out of his mind what the boss said about Natalya. He was filled with pity for her. Had he known more of life and known how to dream, he would have made various plans for her salvation. But he knew almost nothing. All his thoughts were concentrated on his different images of her—in the cellar, at the hospital, drunk up there in the squalid attic room. He moved her from place to place. He would take her, drunk, from the attic and lead her to the hospital, to his cot. Then, in his mind, there would evolve an absurd picture which depressed him. But when he imagined her in the attic as she was when she visited him in the hospital, his mood changed. He would look about him smiling, smiling at the dark street, at the sky studded with golden stars.

Two waves pounded inside him; one warmed him, the other, cold, sad, enveloped him in heavy gloom. He had thought about Natalya so much and so constantly in the hospital that he felt a kinship with her. She was the first person to be kind to him, to care for him. His empty, lonely life, a life without a point of support, without a friend, immediately had concentrated wholly upon her, this girl who had been good to him, who now must be condemned.

He recalled the feeling that had excited him when she sat near his cot. He would have liked this feeling, already somewhat dimmed in recollection, to be reborn with the same intensity as then.

He heard a loud exclamation. "Oh, it's you! When were you let out?" He turned quickly and saw her. She stood at the gate. Her head and face were tightly wrapped in a gray shawl but he could see her large blue shining eyes.

"I got out yesterday. Hello!" he answered, and, not knowing what else to say, he looked at her in silence.

"How thin you are! Ai, ai, ai!" she said slowly

163

in pity, adjusting her shawl to cover more of her face.

"I heard you were ill too," said Paul.

"I? No-o-o, that is, yes, why, even now I'm not quite well. I've had a bad toothache . . . for a long time."

Paul remembered that up in the attic, when she passed him, her cheek had not been bound up.

"Everything all right now? Are you well? Are you working again?" she asked after a pause.

"I'm working. I began right away, yesterday."

"Well, good-by," and she stretched her hand out to him.

Paul took her hand, pressed it tightly, and, not wanting her to leave so soon, said hurriedly:

"Wait a minute. Please! Sit down here. I want to thank you very much. I humbly thank you for worrying so much about me . . ."

"Oh, go on! That's nonsense . . . How would you like to come over and have tea with me some time—during the day, at dinner time. I'm not usually home in the evenings. Come, will you?"

"I'll come. I surely will. With pleasure! Thank you!"

"Well, I'll run up to the store." and she was off.

Paul waited for her return in the vague hope that perhaps she would stop again, perhaps invite him to come up to her place right away; but she hurried past, not looking at him. It seemed to him that she was carrying bottles under her shawl.

He sighed, sat there a little longer, and then went to bed. He thought about her sadly. For a long time he could not fall asleep.

Two days later he walked up the stairs leading to her attic, carrying a kerchief wrapped in paper. He had paid a ruble and a half for it. The door was open. When she saw Paul, Natalya rushed back into the room, grabbed her shawl, wrapping it quickly about her head.

"Oh, it's you! Now that's good. I was just about to have tea. Hello. Hel-l-o!"

In silence he shoved his gift into her hands and murmured softly:

"This is for you . . . in thanks . . ."

"What is it? Oh, a kerchief! Oh, what a nice one! Oh, you, you're a dear!" she said slowly, and moved toward him, extending her arm as if wishing to embrace him. But she restrained herself and fell to admiring the kerchief.

Paul saw that his gift was appreciated and beamed. He watched her turn the kerchief about in front of her, once this way, once that. Suddenly obeying a coquettish impulse, she turned to a small mirror hanging on the wall. With a deft movement of her hands, she unwrapped the shawl and threw his gift on her head.

"My God!" Paul exclaimed.

Tremendous blood-red bruises shone under both her eyes. Her lower lip was swollen, apparently the result of heavy blows.

Paul's exclamation made her remember, but it was already too late. She slumped into a chair and covered her face with her plump white hands.

"The rascals! How they beat you!" escaped from Paul's lips like a heavy sigh.

Heavy silence ensued. Paul was bewildered. He looked around the room, unable to speak, unable even to think of anything to say. The weight of his confusion and grief distorted his pock-marked, thoughtful face into a sort of monstrous yet pitifully sick, yellow mask.

The samovar was boiling on the table. Thin curls of steam were streaming out, melting in the air, leaving no trace. There was a strange, hissing sound as if a small, mean animal were whistling, jeering in cold triumph.

The room had been swept. It no longer seemed turned inside out. It was simply poor, so poor that it could in no way be considered beautiful, even though the occupant had tried to make it so by covering the holes in the wall-paper with cheap, gaudy pictures, by filling the rotting window-sill with three pots of flowers. The coffin-like shape of the ceiling was oppressive; it seemed as if it would fall at any moment. If it did, the room would be dark—dark as a tomb.

Paul looked at Natalya. Her chest was heaving, her shoulders shaking. He did not know exactly why.

"Perhaps I'd better go . . . Good-by!" he sighed, but did not move, because he really did understand her emotion.

Suddenly she removed her hands from her face, jumped from the chair and threw her arms around his neck.

"No, please don't go. It makes no difference now. You've seen it." She waved her hand before her face. "Oh, how I didn't want you to see! You're so good, so kind, so tender, you don't . . . you don't . . . demand. You're not vulgar—like all the others. When I saw you yesterday, I was glad. Ah! I thought, he's well. And I wanted to ask you to come to see me. But I thought, how can I show him my awful face! Why, he'll go away, he'll spit at me, and that will be the end. So I didn't ask you. Another might have laughed, but not you . . . you dear! Why are you such a dear?"

Dizzied by this outburst of shame, grief and happiness, Paul mumbled, looking at the floor:

167

"No, you know I'm not very . . . that is, I'm really no good. I'm dumb. I can't say the right thing. Now here, for instance. I'm so sorry for you, I feel so close to you. But how to say it? I don't know how. I can't even find the words. I've never heard them in all my life. No one . . . never . . . the words I need . . . need now. . . ."

"You pet! He says such wonderful things and thinks he can't talk! Well. Let's sit down. Come over here, beside me. Let's have tea. Wait, I'll close the door. Otherwise some jackass might break in. Well, the devil with all of them! May they all be dropped into Hell! Oh, if only you knew how many skunks there are among your brothers! Go-o-d Lord! It sickens you when you meet them after. . . . They're so nasty, such rascals!"

She became excited. She spared neither "your brothers" nor "my sisters." She appeared to have a great critical talent, a fiery, picturesque style, somewhat sharp, it is true, but this merely heightened the effect. She threw out observations, like stones, and piled them up in paradoxical conclusions, weighty, overpowering.

A life, of which he had no previous inkling, was vividly depicted for Paul. It was such a cursed, filthy, tortuously absurd life that a cold sweat broke out on his brow. He was in terror of such a life, and also of the narrator.

And in truth, the narrator was terrible in her excitement. Her eyes, because of the bruises under them, were unusually deep and shone with wild pleasure in vengeful fury. Her face seemed to be all eyes. Only the swollen lower lip, bared to show her small, sharp teeth, interfered with the illusion. She spoke with icy sadness and ridicule about herself; with vengeful enthusiasm of the misfortunes of "your brothers" and with furious regret at their successes. Sometimes she laughed, sometimes she cried, and sometimes she fused laughter and tears into one. Finally, exhausted and hoarse, she stopped, herself surprised by the effect of her speech.

Paul had lost the look of a human being. His eyes glared. His teeth gnashed savagely; they were clenched so tightly that his cheekbones protruded sharply. His whole face resembled the snout of a hungry wolf. He leaned toward Natalya, but was silent. When she had completed her revelations and complaints, and was already trying to think of some way in which to bring him out of his coma, he came out of it himself.

"Well!" he shouted. "Well! And I didn't even know about such things!" This was said as if now, that he did know, the situation would cease to exist;

he would see to it. "Is that the way things are! My God! Is it possible!" His head dropped on his hands. Elbows on the table, he again was lost in abstraction.

Then Natalya began to speak in a softer, more conciliatory tone. Now she found it possible to excuse and justify herself and others. She tried to foist all the blame for what had happened on drink, a power which destroys all. But she soon found that vodka was too liquid a foundation for all of life's evils and again she fell to accusing people. Having given them their due, she passed on to life.

"You see, it's difficult to live. Pitfalls everywhere. You get around one, you drop into another. There you have it. So you blind yourself and off you go, wherever the crooked lane takes you. Where is the straight path to an easy life? Who can find it? Our life is filthy and hard. But it's not any sweeter for the married ones. It's bad enough to have a kid, but besides there's a husband, pots and pans, and the devil knows what else. Life is so messy!"

Paul listened and visualized life as a series of pits, among them a narrow path along which walked blindfolded man; and the dark, staring pits jeered, filling the air with a putrid, stupefying stench; lone, weak man, his head whirling, reeled, and fell. . . .

His lecturer had switched to a minor, philosophical key. She was talking now about something strange; of graves, of wormwood growing on them, of the dampness of the earth, of stuffiness . . .

Paul felt that in a moment he would begin to cry. It was time to go.

"I'm going. Good-by," he said briefly. She did not try to stop him. In farewell she merely said just one tender "come soon," to which he nodded.

He went out into the street. For a long time he roamed about the town, feeling he had matured this evening. He felt somehow bigger and heavier because he now carried within himself so many new thoughts, conceptions, feelings. Everything around him, the whole town, seemed new, aroused suspicion in him, lack of trust, a contemptuous sad pity. This, one must assume, arose from the fact that Paul had that day learned of the mysteries of many districts of the town.

He walked all night and returned home with the rising sun.

7

A week went by. Paul visited Natalya exactly seven times.

Conversations about life in general and about their own lives gave both of them much pleasure. Paul could now make real the dream he had in the hospital. He told Natalya about taciturn Arefi, about his own thoughts when, as a boy, he used in lie in the ditch near the bathhouse; how, later on, he bummed around the cemetery, the town, and the surrounding villages. All these thoughts bore an imprint of bewilderment, of a lack of trust in himself. But the main tenor of them was that there was something wrong about life, that there was something broken requiring substantial repair.

She told him her biography, a very simple one. When she was sixteen, working as a maid in the home of a merchant, she was sinned against quite unexpectedly. Her parents drove her out of the house. They were petty bourgeois named Krivtsov. Like all people with no place to go, she found herself on the street. A benefactress appeared. Then—a benefactor. Another benefactor. Still another. Then there came a wave of benefactors—the devil knows where from! And they had continued to be plentiful for eight years—up to the present. With a sigh, she frankly confessed all. But Paul already knew about the benefactors. The story merely made him sad, without arousing any specific reaction from him.

There was established between them a simple, friendly attitude. She often spoke to him as she would to a woman. And he spoke to her as he would to a man. The bruises gradually faded. Her face began to acquire its natural, healthy, rosy color. She was robust. The thin, leaden pallor, typical mark of her profession, was not yet evident on her cheeks. She loved to sing and often sang very foolish, sad songs which invariably dealt with unrequited love.

But apparently the word love did not evoke in her any especially pleasant associations and sensations. Even a seventy year old woman would not have been able to equal the coldness and the indifference with which she pronounced the word. For in an old woman, this word at least recalls memories and a sigh for the past.

She simply liked Paul, which was entirely natural. He was the first man who did not approach her, and could not approach her, as had all other men before him. She understood that he was decent to her—as to a woman—and this elevated her somewhat, made her better. His attitude made it unnecessary for her to play a vulgar part—be brazen. Nor was it necessary for her to resort to a cynicism which had not yet managed to become a part of her. At the same time, she could speak to him about everything quite simply, and he, although he spoke little himself, always listened attentively.

He began to loosen up and speak more than he had previously. This again was natural, for she tried to understand him, his soul, his thoughts. He was dear and necessary to her. He was amazed. She seemed to him exceptionally good and kind and soft; and yet she was one of those about whom he had never heard a good word.

He often thought of Arefi. Paul began to wonder

who was the finer person, Arefi or Natalya. He did not permit himself to reply to that question; the answer might have insulted the memory of the deceased, might not have been to Arefi's advantage. The evenings were inexpressibly pleasant to Paul. For then, having finished his work, he would come to her place, freely, simply. They would sit, drink tea, and converse without a care.

She loved to read touching little stories, printed on cheap paper, that sold two for five kopeks. She had a whole pile of them in a trunk under her bed. Sometimes she read one of these to Paul, and, having read it with enthusiasm, she would try to persuade him to get to like reading, which he always promised to do.

Paul felt relaxed, at ease, and even learned to laugh, which, incidentally, did not become him. Miron would look at him good-naturedly and snicker; sometimes he would laugh slyly. However, Paul was not the least affected by this. He grew to like his boss all the more. Miron became increasingly attentive to Paul's affairs. Paul repaid him for this by working like an ox.

One day the boss said:

"Well, Paul, how about taking me with you sometime?"

Curiously enough, Paul welcomed this proposal.

And one evening, the two of them sat drinking tea in Natalya's attic. The old man kept a vigilant eye on the youngsters, letting them talk and only occasionally edging two or three little joking words into their conversation.

They spent the evening very happily and pleasantly. Going home with Paul, Miron at first mumbled something through his teeth. Then he said, touching Paul's shoulder:

"You're a funny guy, brother. And she, too—well, she's a girl. If only you two don't accidentally squeeze each other's tails, everything will be all right."

Paul understood nothing. But, sensing that this was said with good intent, he thanked the boss. In bewildering situations, he always resorted to thanks.

Once, when Paul and Natalya were sitting, and, as usual, having tea—they were both great ones for tea drinking—they talked about who likes what. Paul enumerated his likes and dislikes. Then he listened quietly to Natalya's list.

She named many things. Merry-go-rounds, cognac with lemonade (she liked it even more with seltzer), the circus, music, songs, books, the autumn (because it is very sad), little children (before they have learned to be wicked), meat dumplings, and so on, and finally, she concluded, boats.

"That I like more than anything else," she confided, her eyes shining. "You ride in one and it rocks you like a baby in a cradle. And so you become a baby; you don't understand anything, you think of nothing, you ride and ride. . . . I could ride on forever, on and on, right out to the sea, all my life. That would be good. Oh, for a ride!"

And so they decided to go for a boat-ride on Sunday. The weather happened to be good—clear, warm July weather. They chose a light, solid boat. Paul sat at the oars; they pulled out against the current. On one side the shore was bordered by a wide brown ribbon of clay-covered cliff. On the other, there was a fringe of green bushes from which rose, here and there, sumptuous tall birches, high as the heavens, silvery poplars, and monstrously wind-blown oaks, bent downward by their branches. Behind the boat ran the rippling and undulating foam, with a lost, hurt, discontented sound because it could not overtake the boat. The sky, clear and deep, was reflected in the water, as were those bushes which grew close to the shore, their shadows lying just below the surface of the water. The bushes rocked back and forth in lazy beatitude and grace, as if pleased with themselves.

Bold, brisk swifts flew busily over the water. Wagtails strutted along the shore, swinging their black tails ridiculously, as if they were small crows. The foliage trembled as the river splashed against the shore; somewhere in the distance a song drifted, strong, chesty, beautiful; full, soft sounds were carried over the river.

In a red shirt, his head bare, Paul rowed powerfully and evenly, like an experienced oarsman, working only the muscles of his arms. Sometimes a strand of hair fell across his forehead and he tossed it back with an easy motion of the head. His eyes shone with pleasure; he breathed deeply of the dry, fragant air, occasionally saying, "Oh, how beautiful!"

Natalya sat across from him, her hands on her knees, a heavenly smile on her lips. She rocked in rhythm with the dip of the oars in the water. Beautiful shining drops fell quietly from the oars, caressing the surface of the river. Natalya looked around, at the oarsman, strong and big, and a smile spread from her pensive, tender blue eyes, to her lips, full and luscious.

Neither of them wanted to speak. Both felt that everything was better without words. They were very like the hero and heroine of a popular romance — as yet they were only slightly in love, not yet conscious of that love, but already they were sufficiently interested to watch each other closely — a process which hastened the development of events.

179

But Paul and Natalya only resembled that hero and heroine, they had not yet become them, owing to reasons known only to Fate.

"Shall we row toward the shore?" Paul asked when they had bobbed close to a grass plot on the opposite side. This spot had apparently been built by Nature especially for small picnics. It was entirely shaded by the birches which half surrounded it. Soft, low grass studded with common flowers covered it.

They got out, taking with them a small package of food, a metal teapot and a bottle of something to drink. In half an hour a fire was blazing on the grass plot. Over it hung the teapot. From time to time, drops of water fell from the side of the pot into the fire and evaporated, sizzling. The smoke twirled in dove gray, curly garlands, melting in the air, intoxicating the small midges which, buzzing lazily, fell to the ground.

Everything was very still, as if attuned to listen. Paul bustled about, untying the package. Natalya, with the face of a dreamer, was picking flowers and blades of grass; quietly singing, she made bouquets. This is sentimental, but it was so. Natalya gathered flowers, breathed their fragrance, just like any young girl. I beg forgiveness of all other girls for placing my heroine on the same plane with them. Believe me, this is not my intention! Let them be calm. I would not dare to compare them with my heroine. I am not an idealist. I am merely convinced that all people can be good if they so wish and if they have enough leisure to devote to being good.

Then the teapot began to boil and they had tea and snacks. They were careful to offer tidbits to each other and exchange short remarks on how good everything was. Paul's head began to hum after three classes of "that something to drink." He felt the need to talk.

"Life must be good for those who understand the way things are," Paul began thoughtfully.

Natalya looked at him, and, after a pause, said: "What's good about it?"

Paul had to think before he could answer. Taking advantage of his hesitation, she said, not waiting for his answer:

"I don't know. But for me, it's better not to understand. The less you ask, the easier it is. Take life as it comes, and pay little attention to other people."

Then they began to philosophize, but they soon tired of it. They chatted. Paul became more and more drunk. Evening came, quiet and warm. Natalya saw that it was dark now; she was sad and wanted to go home. She had a hard time convincing Paul that it was time to go. Although he agreed with her, he felt limp all over and did not budge. He grinned foolishly and showed obvious signs of a weak struggle with his overpowering drowsiness.

At last she was able to lead him to the boat, where he immediately stretched out in the bottom and fell asleep. She took up the oars. The boat moved with the current, quietly slid along, close to the shore. A breeze blew their bonfire apart. The sparks fell on the water and on the shadow cast by the bushes along the bank.

Natalya directed the boat toward the middle of the river. In the soft light of the faint moon, she regarded sleeping Paul in silence, but she must have been thinking of something sad for the tears rolled down her cheeks. On one shore there were clumps of bushes, on the other, a sharp precipice. In the sky, the stars shone clearly. Silence. It was as if all the living had fallen into deep slumber. Even the water under the boat made no sound; dark and calm, it seemed as thick and smooth as butter. The lights of the town blinked in the distance and a hollow noise came from there, at first intermittently like the moan of some sleeping animal, then in a solid continuous wave.

When they arrived the boat bumped hard against the shore and Paul awoke. He was ashamed that he had slept.

182

"Forgive me, Natalya, for such a . . ." he said when they had already walked some distance from the shore along the deserted, narrow street.

She was surprised:

"What for?"

Then, firmly, he explained that it was not proper to sleep in front of a lady.

"Good God!" she exclaimed. "Where did you get that? Such nonsense—where did you get it?"

"It's not nonsense," he insisted. "You read that from a book yourself. Don't you remember?" And he recalled the passage to her. "There, you see!" He was proud of being right and added: "Why, there can't be nonsense in books!"—from which one can see how limited was his acquaintance with literature.

When they reached home, he stopped at the foot of the stairs leading to the attic. Extending his hand he said "Good-bye." She hesitated. Then suddenly she seized his hand and pressing it tightly with both her own, murmured in a strange tone:

"My dear! How sweet you are! How sweet!"

She ran upstairs quickly, leaving him somewhat bewildered at her praise.

Soon they arranged another pleasant boat-ride...

And that is how it went.

But just as people become bored, Fate evidently

tired of this idyllic interlude, so she transformed it into a real romance.

This is how it began:

One evening, a sweet, mustachioed countenance glanced into the door of the shop and very politely asked Paul:

"Permit me to inquire, does a young lady named Natalya live here? Natalya—er—er—."

It would have been better for the face not to have asked. After the question, it became transformed Paul's eyes into a revolting mug.

"I don't know," he answered dully and not too pleasantly.

"You know, a kind of blonde, with blue eyes, not tall."

"I don't know," Paul repeated, now definitely unpleasant.

"Er — er — they told me, that here," the questioner hesitated, disappointed. "Excuse me, goodby."

Paul did not answer. Although the man was already gone, he still felt the urge to throw a boottree at his head.

"Do you know whether a girl named Natalya lives here?" the polite, rich baritone came from the yard.

Paul, boot-tree in hand, jumped up, ran to the

door. But when he reached it, Natalya's voice rang out:

"This way, this way, Yakov Vasilich!"

Paul turned back, sat down, shoved his awl into the wrong spot, threw the shoe on the floor, and started again for the yard. He stood on the threshold and looked up at the window. He could see nothing but he heard her voice, her happy voice, and the man's, deep, ingratiating. Then there were steps on the stairway. They both came out. Paul quickly shut the door. Leaving a little crack open, he put his eye up against it.

Natalya walked along with the tall man in a gray derby. He was twirling his mustache and looking into her face. She cast a sidelong glance at the door behind which Paul stood. They left.

Paul went back into the shop and sat at the window. In order to be able to see the street, he threw his head back. But he could see only the top floor opposite, the roof and the sky. For the first time, he felt buried in the ground, below the surface, here in the deep, damp, smoky basement. His head dropped. He was sunk in thought. The boss came and talked to him, but did not receive an answer. He asked in a sympathetic tone:

"What's the matter? You look as if you could eat nails!"

"Oh!" Paul said. His glance was gloomy, searching.

"I'd swear it was Natalya who just rode by in a carriage with some no-account," the boss announced.

"No, it wasn't."

"No? Then why don't you go to see her?" Miron inquired, looking at his worker suspiciously and curiously.

"I'm going now."

And he did indeed go to the attic, but the door of Natalya's room was locked. He sat on the top step and looked down into the dark pit of the staircase, yawning silently and forbiddingly before him.

Down below somebody was talking, but Paul could not follow what was said. He was engrossed in one problem only: How to prevent Natalya from playing around with these swells in derby hats. The one before this wore a derby hat too, but it was a black one, and he had a reddish, sparse beard instead of a mustache. He too resembled a devil shorn of his fur. Paul thought: why are such men born, and why do they live? Why aren't they condemned to exile at hard labor? Paul was perplexed, unable to answer these questions, and others of like nature. He had been free of his melancholy for a long time; now it reappeared. Therefore the feeling was more intense, and he also felt hurt, which was equally painful to bear.

Oppressed, he waited for one hour, two, until dawn. At last he heard the jarring sound of a droshky stopping at the gate. There were steps in the courtyard.

A shudder ran through him. He started to leave, but it was already too late. Natalya, pale, eyes dull in a crumpled face, came up the stairway. She saw him and stopped, halfway, embarrassed by his presence.

"Oh, it's you! Why?" she began, but after looking at him, stopped talking.

He was dry, tense, haggard from lack of sleep, unnerved by the thoughts that had been passing through his mind all night. His eyes frightened her; there was a look in them she had never seen before.

She was not so much ashamed as afraid. Leaning on the railing, she could go no farther; and he, gazing at her stubbornly, did not move. The scene was wordless and strained exaggerated by the light which fell, in a shaft, from the dormer-window in the roof. It fell on him, then, continuing down the staircase, touched her, changing her expression from one minute to the next.

Paul would probably have been very much surprised had he been able to see himself. He sat, elbows on knees, palms supporting his chin, looking down like a judge. The situation was tense and became more oppressive with each succeeding moment. Neither moved. She paled more and more and began to shake under his stubborn, condemning gaze. It seemed to her that his sharp, keen, pock-marked face was becoming more intense, more inflamed with hate and cruelty. No one knows how this difficult situation might have ended had not a cat come to the aid of the pair. The cat, spitting, jumped through the dormer, leaped over Paul, then on down the stairs under Natalya's feet, and disappeared.

I invoke neither good nor evil spirits. I am governed by one spirit alone, the spirit of truth. I produce a cat, one of those minor accidents which appear and disappear but which often clear the path for major events. These little incidents are rarely noticed. I cannot tell you the size and color of this respectable cat to which I am indebted for so simply extricating Paul and Natalya from a most difficult situation.

With a cry, Natalya ran up the stairs past Paul, and he jumped aside.

"Damned cat, how she frightened me!" Natalya whispered, panting, rattling the lock on the door.

Paul was shaken, too. Both of them had now been

jolted out of their stupor. Opening the door of the room, Natalya invited him in.

He walked in silently. He had the appearance of a man who has come to an important decision. He sat on a chair by the window while she unfastened an old-fashioned lace shawl pinned to her shoulder.

"Why did you get up so early to-day?" she asked, feeling that silence was imminent, that again a tense situation was once more in the making.

He looked at her gloomily. Then as if prodded from within, he said, heavily and haltingly:

"I haven't been to bed yet. Yesterday, when I saw that m-m-mug with you, I simply—it's impossible! You must quit this kind of life! Do you think it's good? Everybody can do as they want with you. Really, you were not born into the world for this! It's not decent! Not decent! Can it be pleasant for you? Is it possible? A man comes, takes you, leads you away—and all that. No, you stop it! Stop it, please, Natalya."

He blurted out the last words in a quiet, pleading, supplicating whisper. She was apparently not expecting such an outburst and stood still, her face flushed, clutching her shawl. Her lips moved without making a sound, ridiculously. She evidently had something to say, but was not able, or could not decide whether to speak.

He looked at her, lowered his head, and, having waited for a reply, repeated in the same pleading tone:

"Natalya?"

She moved close to him, put her hand on his shoulder and said sadly, with quiet, bitter conviction:

"Now look! If that's the way it is, I won't lie to you. I'll tell you everything, just as it is. I'll tell you. I know that all this is not pleasant for you, the things I do. Oh, I know it! But what am I going to do? You know it's my living. I'm not fit for anything else. Work? I don't know how to work and I don't like it. Would it be better to work and to starve? But I do have shame—even here with you I'm ashamed. Deeply ashamed, believe me! But—what is there for me to do? Nothing else to do. I have to lead this kind of life — and I will. You know, here's what I'll do. I'll move to another apartment and I won't tell you where. Forget me. What do you need me for? You'd better marry a good girl and live with her. There are good girls for you!"

The last resembled a question more than a statement of fact.

Paul shook his head emphatically.

"We're not talking about the same thing! Not at all! The main problem is you, not I. What am I?

I'm all right. But you must give up this life. It's very filthy! Just look! He came, he led you away—phui! And they're scoundrels. How can they be like that! It makes your hair stand on end when you think about it! Lice!"

"Dear, that's the way it has to be," her tone was appeasing as she stroked his shoulder. She was a little frightened by the bitter distress evident in his words, and by his face, distorted with disgust and hate.

"N-n-nothing *has* to be! You're lying to me. I'm not a baby. You don't need to. I've thought about it. Give it up, you must give it up!"

"My pet, what can I do?" she asked in a quiet, conciliatory tone, more and more frightened, bending over him still farther.

Leaning back on the chair, one hand on the window sill, he gestured with the other, wiping his sweating, hate-inflamed face.

"It must be done! It must be done! Give it up! Chase them all out of here! To hell with them!"

"Don't yell, they'll hear. Stop yelling. Let's talk quietly. Just think. . . ."

"I won't! I've already thought."

"No, just wait a minute."

And, gathering all her courage, she caught his hand. Since there was nothing to sit on, she fell to her knees before him.

"I'm no good for any work. No one will have me, because I have that kind of identification paper. . . ." she began, underlining each word precisely.

He motioned impatiently. Then suddenly struck by an idea, he froze, bent over her and peering into her eyes, said, calmly and firmly:

"Look, will you marry me? Will you? Will you? Come. I to you—I for you—" his voice sank to a timid whisper, trailed off.

She leaned back; her eyes opened wide. Suddenly she jumped up, embraced him, and began to whisper through her tears:

"Dearie! Sweetie! Pet! Marry me, me—me—me! You! You — I — marry! You're funny — you baby!"

She began to kiss him, her arms tight around his neck, laughing hysterically and crying at the same time.

This was new to him. He was in a fog. At first he could only hear the blood rushing in a torrent through his veins. Then he was overcome and eagerly pressed her to him, panting, trying to say something, kissing her face again and again with his hot, hungry lips. . . .

* * * *

The early rays of the sun penetrated the window and filled the bedroom with tender rosy light.

Paul woke first. It was stuffy in the room, blindingly light, and quiet. From the distancec, there came a dull, indistinct noise. The sun shone directly on Natalya's face. Her eyelids were pressed tight, her brows drawn together in a frown. Her upper lip, lifted as if in dissatisfaction, made her look capricious, irritated. Her flushed cheeks made Paul think that she was merely pretending sleep. Her blond hair had become dishevelled in sleep and lay around her in light, beautiful fluffy strands. One plump white shoulder was bare; her thin, rosy nostrils quivered in breathing. All of her was somehow translucent in the sun; she glowed.

Paul, lying beside her, began gently smoothing her hair. She opened her eyes sleepily, smiled at him very affectionately, and turned away from the sun.

Paul got up and dressed. Then, carefully, without a sound, he set a chair down by the bed, sat in it and again began to look at her—listen to her even breathing. She seemed so near to him, so akin, so dear, as never before. He smiled and began to plan and dream of their future—as is appropriate for a happy lover, one not yet tired of his love.

He imagined the shop he would open when they were married. It would be a small room; not dark and sooty like Miron's, but light and clean. Next to it, there would be another room, their room; also small but hung with blue wall-paper, while the first one would be done in yellow with red flowers. That would be very beautiful. The windows of the apartment would face the garden where they would have tea in the evening. In the summer, the wind, carrying the lush smell of greenery, would blow gently into the room. She would cook, he would teach her to sew boots, they would have children. And there would be other such good, quiet, lovely things.

Paul rose, completely happy, sighing deeply. He went up to the table, picked up the samovar, and taking it out into the hallway, began to stoke it. He smiled broadly. How lucky of him to think of it! She would get up, and the samovar would be bubbling busily on the table. He would be sitting beside it, playing housekeeper! She would praise him . . .

When the kindling burnt down, he added coal, then, stepping carefully, he walked back into the room, intending to put everything in order. But Natalya was already awake and his dream picture was shattered. She was lying in bed, her arms behind her head, yawning in the most prosaic manner. Her face had no special expression, except that it was obvious she knew Paul well — very well. He was distressed.

194

"I've put up the samovar," he announced with some regret.

"Yes? What time is it?"

"Past noon."

It frightened him that they were speaking about such things. The way he felt, they ought to be talking about something entirely different, but about what, he could hardly have said. He sat down again near her bed.

"Well, how do you feel?" she asked with a smile.

"Oh, I feel so good, Natasha. So good!" he exclaimed, enraptured.

"Well, that's fine," she said with a little laugh.

Paul wanted to kiss her. He lifted her head, stooped over her.

"Oh! I see you did like it!" Again she laughed her little laugh.

Her words and laughter chilled Paul.

"What are you saying?" he asked, confused.

"I? I, nothing, Just so. Do you still want to marry me?"

Paul sensed the suspicion and ricidule in her tone. What could it mean?

She began to dress, sitting on the bed. Her face was sad and somewhat cruel.

"What has come over you?" Paul asked timidly.

"Why?" she asked without looking at him.

Paul did not know precisely. He felt only that she was not what she should have been in this situation. But she had her own reason for being exactly as she was. When she awoke, a sharp change had taken place in her. She remembered everything that had happened between them. She remembered, and felt that she had lost a dear friend by yielding to an impulse which placed their relationship in the familiar, boring, dirty frame. She had enough of that. What she had liked in Paul was his respectful and friendly attitude. This had still existed a few hours back. Now, it seemed to her, it must disappear. She knew very well how such relationships end. They always began in the same way. Although she saw that Paul was happy, joyful, she could not imagine he would remain so for long. She had lost a friend. She was angry with herself. Her heart was filled with grief. Paul had not yet toppled from his throne, but she could not help reading into his actions something of her own feeling.

Watching as she dressed, he felt more and more agitated by a passionate desire to embrace and caress her. Feeling no necessity for restraint, and he had not the strength for such restraint, he did embrace her. She submitted to him with an indifferent and wry little smile. She was cold, but he, filled with fire enough for both of them, did not notice. . . .

196

Ten minutes later they were having tea; she already washed and combed, sat on the bed; he, on the chair facing her. He was filled with quiet enthusiasm and fatigue. She was sad, looked at him over the saucer of tea, and sighed.

Suddenly Paul noticed that big tears were rolling down her cheeks, dropping into the tea which she continued to drink. Hardly anyone ever drank tea with tears and yet managed to appear so calm and indifferent as this unpredictable girl.

"What's the matter with you, eh? What happened? What's it all about?" Paul said quickly, jumping from his chair and rushing toward her.

She banged the saucer on the table, splashing her teary tea. Sobbing, she began:

"I'm a fool! I've robbed myself! For once in my life I heard a nightingale, and I've frightened it away! I fixed it! You're done for, Natasha! Now I'll eat my heart out. Oh! Oh! Oh! Fool! Fool!"

Paul did not understand. His caresses only heightened her suspicion. She continued to cry. Finally, he said:

"Well, enough, Natasha! Stop it. We'll get married, and then we'll really begin to live! I'll have my own shop and you'll be a housekeeper, a wife, like all the other women. It will be so nice."

197

She pushed his arm away. Sardonically, yet with a faint, barely acknowledged hope, she said:

"For how long? You'll talk like that for a week. We know you! Ah, we know, my boy. I didn't mean that. I wasn't thinking of that. Don't be afraid. I won't take your proposal seriously. I won't accept it. No. Do you really think I'd marry you? I won't marry anyone, not even you. And you're good. Good doesn't last long. I don't want to hear reproaches for my past life. I won't! You think you won't remind me what I've been if I become your wife? Oh, brother! You'll do it like anybody else. I know it. For the likes of me there isn't one dry spot in the whole swamp of life. But let's not talk about that. I don't want your proposal. What I regret, fool that I am, is that you are no longer my friend. And I myself am to blame. Oh, oh! I'm a fool!"

Paul tried hard to understand her, but could not. Her tears affected him, aroused in him a melancholy, a fear of something intangible.

"Listen, Natasha! Don't torment me," he said seriously. "Don't torture me with those words. I can't understand them. I don't get them. But the words are not the whole trouble. I'll say this, I'm ready to turn my whole heart inside out for you. Look! You're the dearest person in the whole world to me. You're the very dearest. That's how I feel. I'll

do anything for you. Tell me, 'Paul, put out the sun!'
I'll crawl out on the roof and blow on the sun until
I either put it out, or burst. Say to me, 'Paul, cut up
people!' I'll go and cut them up. Say, 'Paul, jump
out of the window!' I'll jump. I'll do anything you
want. Say, 'Paul, kiss my feet!' I'll do it this very
minute. Shall I? Let me!''

He threw himself at her feet.

Natalya was overcome by this outburst. She listened to his first words with an incredulous smile.
She laughed quite gaily when he suggested putting
out the sun. She shuddered when, in her honor, he
wanted to cut up people. He was terrifying, all
aflame and trembling. And when he wanted to kiss
her feet, she felt a wild pride, and, not objecting,
allowed him to do so.

To enslave a man has always been a great pleasure
for anyone. Here was a man enslaved by her. But
another human quality was not foreign to her—that
of pity—and she pitied Paul at her feet. She bent
over, lifted him from the floor, lifted him and caressed
him in a way she had not caressed anyone before.
Finally, they were both worn out and exhausted.

But they were not yet completely calm. They decided to go for a stroll in the field on the outskirts of
the town. Paul forgot the shop, the boss, everything,
and walked with her along the narrow deserted

streets which she chose deliberately, fearing to meet acquaintances. They wandered alone in the field for a long time. They spoke frankly, unafraid to appear funny or foolish to each other, not wanting to force their respective ideas and feelings on each other, with no desire to show supremacy one over the other, with none of those attitudes which enter into the love of cultured people and are supposed to make love more piquant, but less wholesome.

Let us then forgive our hero and heroine their lack of culture "on the grounds of the above-mentioned circumstances", as the jurists say.

Finally, they came to the river, sat under the willows by the shore, on the sand washed by the waves. After a while, they fell asleep, locked in each other's arms.

8

After a few days Paul thought that every pair of masculine feet passing by the window of the shop were on their way to Natalya's attic. He jumped up each time and ran into the courtyard. The boss watched—Paul had already told him everything— and snickered into his beard. When Paul had respect- fully requested the boss to be the one to bless the married couple at the ceremony, Miron was struck dumb. When he recovered, he delivered a speech.

"Fool! You listen to me. I've been married twice.

My first wife couldn't tell the difference between me and the other fellows in the shop. My second loved me so much I don't know how I came out alive. She would wallop me with whatever came to her hand, whenever she pleased. She liked to beat people up so much you would have thought her father and mother were cops."

Then he pictured family life completely; pots and pans, diapers, pokers, washing clothes, washing floors, and all the other conveniences. According to his description—and he swore to its truth—there was soap in his cabbage, he had to walk on his hands, wet diapers slapped at him, and his wife tested the strength of the various pots by tossing them at his head. Finally, Miron switched to the subject of women, and came to a sad conclusion.

"You're a queer duck! There are plenty of women. What do you need this one for? You'll just ruin yourself with her. Take it from me. Let's suppose she has done you some good. All right, now you're a man, you're gay, you laugh, you make conversation. But my dear fellow you've already repaid her. Who else would treat her the way you do? Well, she's had enough of that. If you want to marry, then get married right. I'll pick out a nice, plump girl for you. That'd be the thing for you. There'd be a dowry, you'd open your own shop. But not with this

202

one! In a month you'll be fed up. And how will you live? You have nothing—no cups, no spoons. She doesn't know how to do anything. Spit on her; she's no good!"

The speech had as much effect on Paul as on the walls of the shop. Paul was so attached to Natalya that far from the thought of dismissing her, he felt her presence was necessary to him every minute; he wanted her in the shop so that he might be able to work as intensely and attentively as he used to.

Once, after work, he did not find her at home when he went to visit. He paled, trembled, and sat at the door until she arrived. It was well past midnight when she came, yet she was sober and as proper as she could be. She immediately quieted Paul by telling him that she had been visiting a girl friend who had promised to get her a maid's job. He believed her and was glad; he forgot his fears.

Soon after that, however, he began thinking: Where does she get her money? This question gave him the cold shivers. That same evening he asked. She replied with another question:

"How much do I need?"

But he was not satisfied.

"I saved a little, kopek by kopek. That's what I live on."

Something prompted him to say:

"Show me the money!"

She hesitated, and finally said "All right. I can show it. If you wish."

But she could not find the key to her trunk.

The question remained unanswered.

When Paul described his vision of their future life together, she was silent, her eyes closed dreamily. When, transported by his own fantasies, he caressed her, she was cold. Once this was so obvious that he was moved to ask:

"Perhaps you don't like this?"

She was a long time answering; her glance was perplexed. Quietly, as if not quite believing her own words, she finally said:

"N-n-o-o. Why do you think so? I do, very much."

This was enough to calm him.

He began to give her his pay, just as if she were his wife, his housekeeper. Once he brought her material for a dress. Her response to the gift was tender but formal. He experienced the first signs of a keen, sharp jealousy because of her lack of concern for his regard. He had no clear understanding of such feelings, but he knew enough not to express them.

Then one day, when they were having tea, steps and carefree whistling came up the stairway. A thin, tenor voice sang:

'I'm going to my darling Natasha,
    And here's Natasha's n-e-s-t.''

Paul had a premonition that something unpleasant was about to happen. He frowned angrily.

"And here's Natasha's n-e-s-t—So! You have guests!'' the singer concluded, disappointedly pausing at the door.

He was a rather miserable looking dandy with a goatee and small turned up mustaches. Peering at Paul, he entered the room in a casual manner, hung his hat on a hook even more casually, then walked toward Natalya whose welcoming smile was somewhat confused and guilty.

"Hel-l-o-o, heavenly Natasha.''

"What do you want?'' growled Paul.

The dandy looked at him, wiggled his mustaches, and paying no attention to Paul, finished his greeting by taking Natalya's hand gallantly.

"Miss Krivtsov! Treat me to some tea and enlighten me concerning this dirty-faced gentleman with an eye-shade.''

"Beat it!'' said the dirty-faced gentleman, rising from his chair.

"What's that? Natasha, what's the meaning of this?'' said the insulted dandy, addressing his hostess.

"Beat it!'' Paul repeated, shaking with anger.

205

"All right, I'll go," the visitor hurriedly agreed, and he left, shouting as he went down the stairs;

"I wish you a happy legal marriage, Natasha. I'll inform—"

But whom he wanted to inform remained unknown.

They sat for a long time in silence.

Paul asked gloomily:

"When will they stop coming?"

"When you chase them all out," Natalya said placidly.

"Are there many more?"

"I don't know. I never counted them. How come you dislike them so much?" she laughed, sneering.

"I can't stand it! Understand? I can't! You're mine now."

"So that's how it is? Where did you buy me? How much did you pay for such merchandise?"

Paul glowered.

"You laugh. . . . You shouldn't. I'm not lying, you know. You're mine, in the day, in the night. I always think of you, always."

"That's enough. . . . Finished. We'll say no more." Her tone was dry.

For some time, Paul's attitude toward her visitors had disturbed Natalya. She thought it unnecessary to break off with them. Some of them were very nice, gay people. At times she found Paul not only a boor, but anti-social. It would be very difficult for her if he were always to be around. Her tastes were different. His were very strange, almost laughable. But despite all this, he was good, clean, honest; he loved her—she prided herself on that. She was very flattered that he accepted her as an equal. He talked to her freely about everything, and she was able to talk to him in the same way. This was worth a great deal. She began to wonder whether it might be possible to arrange a situation in which she would keep Paul and yet be able to live the life she had been leading. Although she found that sort of life quite unpleasant at times, nevertheless it was often jolly and had its own pleasures. She would like to keep everything nice about it for herself; she was willing to share its evils with Paul. She hoped in time she could tame him sufficiently so that he would accept some such arrangement. She loved to listen to his dreams about marriage. Eyes shut, she would smile, picturing the various scenes of family life, scenes that were happy, lively. She was sometimes carried away by his descriptions. But she was wise enough to know that reality would destroy Paul's fantasies. She was firmly convinced that his passionate love would soon pass. She understood his love in her own way, a way that was not flattering. She was certain that when his love was gone, he would shower reproaches on her, beat her. And besides, it would be very boring to live all her life alone with him, always with the same person in one room, day and night, continually—with just one person.

Then other times, she thought she could live with him nicely and for a long time, but decided it would not be right. She was not worthy of him. She would not agree to marry him merely out of pity; he was such a good person. No, she wouldn't, no matter how many times he asked her. She wished him happiness—but her life must go on in the same way, as it had before.

Such thoughts brought with them an unfamiliar and delicious feeling. She seemed to become cleaner and wiser when she thought this way. Unconsciously impelled by her feminine passion for coquetry, she created artificial moods. When she was with Paul she assumed a quiet, thoughtful, downcast manner. Paul would respond with tenderness. She amused herself in this way and thus managed to dispel some of the boredom she had already begun to feel in her relationship with Paul. But often she could not maintain this role. Then she would hide from him—or show her claws. Paul on the other hand was becoming even more attached to her. More and more frequently, he had the desire to have a decisive conversation with her and finally, this desire was realized.

One evening, strolling about town, they wandered into a small garden. Somewhat tired, they sat on a bench under a thick, overhanging acacia, glistening with the occasional yellow leaves of autumn.

"Well, Natasha, how about it?" Paul asked, looking at her seriously out of the corner of his eyes.

"What about what?" she asked, fanning herself with a broken branch. She had already guessed where this question was leading.

"Well, when will we get married?"

The rays of the moon penetrated through the leaves of the acacia; a lacy shadow fell across both of them. It shimmered on the pathway at their feet, and on the bench opposite. It was quiet in the garden. Over them, in the calm clear sky, transparent feathery clouds slowly dispersed, their fluffy bright texture revealing the twinkling stars.

Tired from their walk, and responsive to the setting, Natalya was in a pensive, thoughtful mood. Her opposition to marriage seemed at this moment genuine, truly felt and thoroughly justified.

"Married?" she shook her head. "Let me tell you. Forget about it. What sort of a wife can I be? I'm just a street walker. And you, you're an honest working man. That's why we're no pair. I've already told you I'm a lost soul. I can't be anything else."

She took pleasure in this self-abasement; she thought of herself as being like one of those heroines in the books she read.

"And you," she continued in a sad tone, "you need a good honest wife. I was doomed from birth to a life of sin. I very much want your life to come out well. A wife. Children. A shop." In a voice trembling with restrained tears, she whispered, "And I shall come quietly to your house and look in and see how my dear Paul—"

She sobbed. In truth, all that she had just said was painful and sad. She remembered a scene from one of her little books: Deeply in love, sacrificing her love for "him" and his happiness, despised by everyone, Marie Désirée, in rags, worn out by a hard life, stands at the window of Charles LeConte, and through the glass sees him, sitting at the feet of his wife Florence, reading a book to her, as she gazes dreamily into the smoking fireplace, one hand holding a child on her knee, the other playing with Charles' hair. Poor Marie had come on foot from afar and brought with her the proof of her innocence and love, but alas! too late! she froze there at the window— How the story ended Natalya never knew; the last pages of the book were torn out. As she recalled this touching story, Natalya sobbed bitterly.

Paul trembled with sympathy and love, helplessness and grief. He pressed her tightly to him. Choked with tears, he said thickly:

"Natasha, darling! Natasha! Enough. Stop it! I love you. I won't give you up!"

Finally she calmed down a little. Agitated by his love of her, and awed by her nobility of soul, which he understood instinctively, Paul said solemnly and firmly:

"Listen to me! You belong to me because I think of you, day and night. There is no one else for me but you. I don't want anyone else. No one. You shall be mine, say what you will! Please, understand, please. I'll give you up to no one. Because there's no life for me without you! How can I live without you when I think of you constantly? You're mine! I'd give my heart for you! Do you understand me? And let's not talk about it any more!"

But she did discuss it. She demeaned herself to him and felt noble. A tremendous sweet feeling took hold of her as she heaped abuse upon herself. Her confessions became more and more candid and cynical. She soon reached the point of saying:

"Do you think that during this time I have been pure? You poor devil, you! Every night—"

211

But she could not finish. Paul straightened up, placed his hands on her shoulders, shook her, and whispered hoarsely:

"Shut up! Shut up! I'll kill you!"

He ground his teeth fiercely.

Natalya was bent back by the weight of his hands pressing on her shoulders; she knew that she had said too much. She was afraid. Paul saw her trembling and pity cooled his passionate jealousy, although it did not lessen the hurt. He slumped down beside her. A heavy silence followed, a long, tiring silence. Natalya, still frightened, was the first to break. She whispered softly:

"Let's go home."

He walked beside her for a while, without a word; Then said, reproachfully;

"You don't love me if you can say such things to me. There is no pity in your words. You should have said nothing."

She sighed deeply; sincere repentance was reflected on her face. Then Paul continued:

"Well, that's that. All right. But in the future, don't say such things to me. We're through talking. I have some money—forty two rubles. The boss owes me nineteen more. That will be enough for us to get married on, and for a little while longer. Do you have a dress, something you could go to church in? One you haven't worn yet—not once?"

"No," she replied, softly.

"Well, you'll have to have one made. I'll get you some material to-morrow."

She said nothing. When they got home, he left her at the stairway, whispering:

"I'm not coming up to-day."

"Very well," she nodded, and ran up the stairs.

He heard the click of the lock and went out into the street. He was deeply hurt by her confessions. The whole street seemed to breathe on him with a strange coldness, arousing long-forgotten feelings, feelings of loneliness, of sorrow. His old thoughts and emotions now seemed much more oppressive, much less understandable; they now possessed a new quality they had not had before.

Natalya locked the door of her room. She did not undress. She sat at the open window and sighed in relief. She looked out the window, her cheek resting on the palm of one hand.

Clouds were gathering. They rose from the dense darkness, covering the horizon with a heavy velvet curtain. They moved slowly, as if long since tired of this job. Enveloping the sky, they extinguished one star after another. Then, as if regretting that they were spoiling the beauty of the sky by erasing its decorations and concealing its soft, peaceful sheen from the earth, the clouds began to weep, large drops of rain. The rain beat down on the iron roof, seeming to send warning signals to the earth.

Natalya, like Paul, was offended. But she felt trapped. "Ah, so that's the kind you are! Just like the others! To-day you love me, to-morrow you'll smash my teeth in! So, my pet! You'll play pranks, hunh! Well, you just wait!"

She remembered his distorted, furious face, the grinding of his teeth, his whispered, "shut up! I'll kill you!" Why? Because she had been so frank, told him the whole truth? Very noble! And he calls himself a friend! He even thinks he loves me.

This was the first time anyone had threatened to kill her. When the others beat her, they beat her for no damn good reason, and always without warning, almost always when they were drunk. Now you take those others—why you can't even compare him to them! Then she fell to thinking of what life with Paul would be, day after day, from morning to night, all the details. She would get up early in the morning. She would still want to sleep, but she would have to put up the samovar. He would have to go to work. She would have to light the stove and cook—if there was something to cook. She would have to clean the room. Then—set the table. Dinner,

214

wash dishes, sweep the floor, sew something for herself or for him, again put up the samovar. Then—evening—

And suppose they go out for a walk, just the two of them—that is, if there is free time. But it's so boring to go walking with him. Hardly anyone would come to see them. He is such a boor and so grumpy. They would return from the walk, have supper, and to bed. That is one day.

But what if he has no work? What if he begins to gnaw at her about her past life? And would he beat her? And then, most likely, he'd be jealous of everyone, from a twelve year old youngster to an old man of seventy. And what would she talk to him about? He is even more stupid than I—he can't read. I like to read books. Where would I get more books?

The more she thought about it, the more boring and distasteful life with Paul appeared.

She put the question to herself, "Why should I sell myself to him?" and quickly found that he really had nothing to offer her in the way of payment. Then she tried to recall just what it was that tied her to him in the first place, in what way she was obligated to him. She discovered, to her great pleasure, that it was he who was indebted to her, not she to him; that her whole attachment to him was based on the fact that he was pitiful, lonely.

And what do I do now? She sighed, felt relieved.
She reproached him energetically:

"Oh, you pock-marked devil! Ha! You just wait.
I'll show you! I'll show you the kind I am! You
won't grind your teeth at me any more! You think
I'm your slave! You've got a lot to learn!

Jumping up, she threw a kerchief over her head.
Not bothering to lock the door, she ran quickly down
the stairs. She did not care that the rain was already
beating down the street, drumming monotonously
on the iron roofs, the pavements, the window panes.
She hurried. She was going to prove to Paul what
sort she was. She was filled with a furious daring, a
consciousness of her independence.

9

She was gone for two days. As soon as Paul entered her room on the morning of the first day, he felt that something new, something unfortunate had happened. He waited for her the whole day. That night, he looked for her around the town. He glanced into all the public houses and taverns. But she was nowhere to be found. He clenched his teeth, frowned and huddled over; was silent all the next day. A dull pain, a premonition of something terrible, something unforeseen, oppressed him. Gradu-

217

ally, his fury against Natalya began to grow. By the third day, he had become thin and hollow cheeked, just as one does after an illness.

On the evening of that day, two carriages passed the shop window and rolled up to the gate. Paul heard her laughter, paled and lunged toward the courtyard.

She clung to the arm of a colorless man in the uniform of a war office clerk. His mustache, face, and jacket, everything about him looked faded. She was tipsy, rolling about, singing and laughing. Behind them walked another couple; a thin, dark girl with a middle-aged man who looked like a cook.

Paul peered from the hall through a crack in the boards. He was boiling inside. He thought he would choke with rage. But when they disappeared up the staircase, he immediately fell into a calm, cold, unmoving despair. He slumped to the floor of the hall, stupefied; his head pressed against a water barrel. He heard laughter and talk, reaching down to him from the attic. Visions of Natalya in various attitudes, lively, laughing loudly, merrily—as she had never been with him—flashed before his eyes.

"Why hasn't she been like this with me?" he thought. Quickly and truthfully, he answered his own question. "With me, Paul, she couldn't be like that. I am awkward, dull, boring." Recognition of this intensified his grief. So it appeared he would lose her. It was his own fault. Lose her! Lose her! And be again as he used to be, lonely, silent, needed by no one, a ridiculous foundling. As always happens when one loves a woman and loses her, Paul recalled all that was best in Natalya. He would not allow himself to think anything bad of her. In the end, he thought of her as so pure, so tender, so kind —she seemed to be so absolutely necessary to him— that his pain increased to the point of suffocation.

Suddenly he jumped up, smiled as if he had come to a bold decision, and plunged through the courtyard. He rushed up the stairs; he was met by a gurgling, rippling sound.

He was at the door. Natalya, excited, flushed, bold, one hand on her hip, the other raised holding a kerchief, was getting ready to dance. Natalya alone was clear, beautiful, alive to him—everything else was in a fog.

"Hello, Natasha!" Paul shouted in a trembling, happy voice.

"Oh! It's—you—dearie! . . ." Her quiet exclamation, frightened, quavering, penetrated through the fog to Paul.

It was dead quiet, everything seemed to float in the fog. Only Natalya stood still, staring, her large blue eyes so kind, so bright.

219

"Yes. Here I've come . . . to you . . . to have a good time. It's merry here. I heard everybody laughing, so I thought I'd come," Paul said, bewildered.

An inner impulse prodded him on so that he stumbled over the threshold to Natalya's feet.

"Natasha! Natasha! I've come. . . . Chase them all out of here! Forgive me! I can't live without you, I can't. I can't! . . . How is it going to be? Alone? It's impossible to live alone! . . . I love you! I love you, you know! Why, I've told you I love you! . . . You belong to me. . . . What do you need those others for? Day and night, day and night, I think only of you. . . . All, all my thoughts. . . . I'll be merry. I'll be gay. I'll laugh. I'll talk a lot. . . ."

He embraced her legs, pushed his head against her knees and mumbled dull, beseeching, pitiful words, so moving that the others were stilled.

Natalya was frightened. She pressed back to the wall, her face pale, distorted. She grabbed his head, tried to push him away with both hands. But he was rigid, clinging to her. Her blue lips moved helplessly, she could say nothing. . . .

Then a weak titter was heard in the room. The dark girl was laughing. The clerk picked up her laughter; then the man who looked like a cook. Natalya, perplexed, turned to them, glanced at Paul

—and burst into laughter herself. The whole attic shook with the loud, hearty guffaws of four people.

Amazed, crushed by this outburst, Paul sat on the floor and stared into the corner with dull, insane eyes. In truth, he did look ridiculous. His face, wet with tears which clung to the pock-marks on his cheeks, was pitiful in its bewilderment. His tousled hair, breaking loose from the band fastened round his forehead, appeared to be some fantastic, clown's wig. Dull eyes, gaping mouth, shirt pulled out of his cobbler's apron, some sort of dirty wet rag sticking to his shoe—all this made it impossible to regard him as a tragic figure worthy of compassion.

Four people doubled up with laughter. He sat on the floor, confused, silent, unmoving. Somebody spilled beer. Thin streams of it ran along the floor toward Paul. The dark girl, in a fit of hysteria, sent a woman's hat flying over his head. It fell on his knees. He took it up, began to examine it in his confusion.

This engendered even more laughter. They laughed, they groaned, they wheezed, they moaned. Paul got to his feet in so clumsy a way he appeared even more ridiculous. He was ridiculous as he staggered to the door. He turned and threw the hat on the floor. He gestured toward Natalya and said, through his teeth:

"Re-mem-ber!" and left, to the accompaniment of unceasing guffaws.

"Oh, what a hero!" someone shouted, laughter turning to tears. "Ohoho! Ahaha! Ha! Ha! Ha! Oh, the devil take him. Ha, ha, ha! Oh, remember that rag around his head! Ha, haha! Hânging down his back like a tail! Oh, hahaha! The hair. Ha, ha, ha, on his head, like a wreath! Ha! Ha! Ha! Oh, may he bu-r-st! Ha! Ha! Ha!"

And outside unceasing rain beat down on the courtyard, monotonous, drumming. It was already Fall.

It rained for three whole days, snapping off the last yellow leaves from the black soaked branches. With the tired, lackadaisical indifference of Fate, the tree tops swayed under the furious beating of the wind, cold, hateful, grief stricken, sweeping along the ground as if in search of something it loved. Stubborn, insistent rain and ceaseless, howling wind created a remarkable requiem for the dying summer; an unusual welcome to the approaching winter. Dense, dull gray clouds covered the sky as if they wished never to part again, as if to prevent the sky from showing itself to the soaked, crumbled earth. On the fourth day, it snowed. The heavy, wet flakes whirled over the town in the wind, the still searching, wildly sweeping wind, pinning the snow to walls and to housetops in white spots.

That evening, Paul crossed the courtyard with the step of a man whose work is done. He moved carefully, trying to keep his boots clean. He walked up the stairs, stood thoughtfully at Natalya's door. He was dressed in his best, clean, his face calm but thin and drawn. He paused, then knocked on the door. Shifting from one foot to the other, he waited for the door to open. He whistled, scarcely audibly, through his teeth.

"Who's there?" a voice asked.

"It's me, Natalya!" Paul answered loudly, calmly.

"Ah!" The door was opened.

"Hello!" Paul greeted her, removing his cap.

"Hello, you funny duck, you! Well? Over it? Oh, how you amused us! What a sight you were! You looked as if they had washed the floor with you! Why didn't you get dressed up then?"

"It never occurred to me. Excuse me!" Paul laughed, looking away.

"Will you have some tea? I'll heat the samovar."

"No, thank you! I have already had some."

Natalya noticed Paul's formal words.

"What's this? Why so distant?"

She laughed contemptuously. Now he was in no way different, in her eyes, from the others. His value

223

had fallen once he had dropped at her feet in front of strangers. She had been beaten before this, more or less cruelly, for unfaithfulness. She expected the same from Paul. But he appeared to be something different. In her opinion, this difference between Paul and the others was not to Paul's advantage. Those fellows beat you—that meant they loved you. When they really love you, they not only beat you, they try to kill you, they go to every extreme. But Paul —he just flopped at her feet in front of strangers and cried like a woman! That's not manly, that's not human! You don't pray, you don't cry, you fight to get a woman. Then she is yours. But perhaps, not even then. . . .

Paul sighed.

"There are no ties between us. There was a friendship between us, but it has already ended. It's over!"

Natalya was surprised, but she concealed it. "Apparently he's come to say good-by." She sat on the bed near him and waited for him to continue.

"It's rather dark here, Natalya. Perhaps you ought to light the lamp . . ."

"All right!" and she did so.

He began to talk, looking thoughtfully at her:

"I'm speaking to you for the last time, Natalya.

224

There will be no chance for us to talk further!"

"How so?" her eyes lowered.

She did not know just how to conduct herself in this situation. She waited for a cue so that she might assume the correct attitude. She noticed how thin he had grown during the past four days. His poise amazed her.

"Why are you talking this way?"

"The time has come for it. I have thought it over, many many times. This must end. . . . Why not? Is there anything more I can expect from you?" he looked at her searchingly.

She regretted what had happened. She pitied him. She sensed that actually, despite his calm, he was unhappy, hurt. She was, after all, a woman. As a woman she could not withhold her pity at the sight of an unfortunate human being.

"What do you mean?" She leaned toward him. "Why, I'm always ready. . . ."

"Oh, no! That's not necessary." He waved her aside. "This is the end. It's finished. You were right. Nothing could have come of it. I see that now. What sort of a husband would I be? What sort of a wife would you make? That's the root of the whole matter. . . ."

He paused.

"What is he driving at?" she thought. She could

not understand. The wet snow slapped softly at the window as if wishing to warn her of something, to remind. . . .

"Yes. I guess you're right. It would have been . . . bad," she whispered very quietly, and felt ever more sorry for him.

"Yes, that's it! But I can't leave you this way. I can't! I've had you in my soul too long. You've meant so much to me. I say it again, of all the people you've been the dearest, closest human being to me. The very dearest. It was with you that I first began to understand life. You've meant a great deal to me. You were the most precious. I must tell you honestly —you've lived in my soul!"

His voice trembled. The tears rolled down her cheeks. She turned away, not wishing him to see.

"You've lived in my soul!" he repeated. "I can't go off and leave you to be ruined, to be dirtied! Never! I can't do that! I can't let a person I love with all my heart, who is more dear to me than anything else, I can't let that person be abused by others. No! I can't, Natalya, I can't!"

Bent over, he tried not to look at her. There was fiery conviction in his voice—and something more, something beseeching, begging, apologetic. His left hand rested on his knee, his right hand in his coat pocket.

226

"What do you mean?" she whispered. She was still turned from him, scarcely able to restrain her sobs.

"This is what I mean! . . ."

Paul pulled a long knife out of his pocket and plunged it into her side with an even, sure hand.

"Ugh!" she gasped weakly and rolled off the bed, directly toward him, her face turned up to him.

He caught her in his arms, placed her on the bed, straightened her dress and looked down at her. Amazement was frozen on her face. Her brows were lifted, her eyes, now dim, were opened wide. Her mouth was half closed; her cheeks wet with tears.

Paul's taut nerves snapped. He moaned dully. He covered her with hot, hungry kisses, sobbing and shaking as if in fever. She was already cold.

The snow slapped at the panes of the window. The wind howled through the chimney, coldly, wildly. It was dark in the courtyard; dark in the room. Natalya's face dwindled to a mere white spot. Paul was paralyzed, bent over her.

For twenty-four hours they were alone. She lay on the bed, a knife in her side. He wept, his head on her breast. Beyond the window the autumn wind, cold, damp, echoed loudly.

They found him thus on the evening of the following day.

10

Spring had already come when the supreme act of man's justice was visited upon Paul Gibly.

The young spring sun came through the window of the hall where the court session was held. It cruelly warmed the smoothly polished bald heads of two gentlemen of the jury. This made them feel a strong desire for sleep. They leaned forward in order to conceal their lethargy from their fellow jurors, the court and the onlookers, thus giving a false impression of extraordinary interest in the proceedings.

One of them examined the countenances of the onlookers very closely. Apparently he did not find a wise face among them for he shook his head sadly. The other twirled his mustache, looked attentively at the secretary who was sharpening a pencil.

Just then the official on the bench announced:

"On the basis of . . . in view of the full consciousness of the accused . . . I assume the interrogation of witness . . ." and turning to the prosecutor asked: "Do you have anything to say?"

This good-natured gentlemen, his mustache like two cockroaches, smiled pleasantly:

"Nothing, Your Honor!"

"Gentleman for the defense! Have you anything to say?"

The defense counsel was no less frank than the prosecutor. He too loudly admitted that he had nothing to say, which was quite evident on his face.

"Accused! Do you have something to say?"

The accused too had nothing to say. He was dull and made a very unpleasant impression on everyone with his pock-marked immobile face.

All three, the prosecutor, the defense attorney, and the accused, cheated those who had come to hear the trial. All—as with one voice—had nothing to say.

The prosecutor had the amazing ability of assuming the savage expression of a hungry bulldog. He also had a strong proclivity for affectation, for intimidation. He threatened to cut the throats of the jury if they dared to be lenient to the accused.

Defense counsel had a habit of blowing his nose in protest as he spoke, of ruffling his hair in a pathetic manner, of crowning his speech with words of pity. He exclaimed eloquently, indignantly, loudly, protestingly:

"Gentlemen of the jury!" He put into this one exlamation all he possessed of pathos, of eloquence. But the rest of his speech was pale, without soul, without appeal to the hearts of the jury. Defense counsel had robbed himself to produce this one salutation.

All during the trial, the accused had had a secret desire. After he was sentenced to twelve years at hard labor, he voiced it loud enough for all to hear.

"I beg your pardon." He bowed to the official; he muttered, beseeching, his eyes moist: "Most Honorable Sir! Can I visit her grave?"

"What?" the official shouted sternly.

"I just want to go to her grave," the accused repeated timidly.

"Impossible!" the official shouted and went off down the corridor with mincing steps.

Two soldiers led the criminal away—in the way criminals are always led from the court room.

How I Became A Writer

HOW I BECAME A WRITER

  The history of human labor and human effort is far more as an individual. For men die, having lived not even a hundred years, but their work lives for many centuries. The fabulous achievements and rapid growth of science is due precisely to the fact that scientists know the history of their own specialty. Science and literature have much in common; in both, observation, comparison and study are of fundamental importance; the artist, like the scientist, needs both

235

imagination and intuition. Imagination and intuition bridge the gaps left in the chain of facts by its as yet undiscovered links and permit the scientist to create hypotheses and theories which more or less correctly and successfully direct the searching of the mind in its study of the forces and phenomena of nature, gradually subjecting them to the human will and thus creating culture, that "second nature" which is our very own, created by our will and our intelligence.

The art of literary creation, the art of creating characters and types demands imagination, intuition, the ability to "make things up" in one's own mind. When a writer describes some shopkeeper, official or workman of his acquaintance he is merely producing a more or less successful likeness of an individual; but such a likeness will remain a mere photograph, without any socially educative significance, and will contribute almost nothing either in width or in depth to our knowledge of life and of our fellow men.

But if a writer is able to extract from twenty or fifty or a hundred shopkeepers, officials or workmen the characteristic traits, habits, tastes, gestures, beliefs, mannerisms typical of them as a class and if he can bring these traits to life in a single shopkeeper, official or workman, he will have created a type and his work will be a work of art. The scope of his observation, the wealth of his experience of life, often endow a writer with the power to transcend his personal subjective attitude to facts. Subjectively, Balzac was an adherent of the bourgeois order but in his novels he exposed the pettiness and baseness of the bourgeoisie with an overwhelming and relentless clarity. There are plenty of instances of writers acting as the unbiased historians of their class and time. In these instances the work of the writer is no less valuable than the work of the scientist who studies the conditions of existence and nutrition of animals, the causes of their multiplication or

236

extinction, and paints a picture of their desperate struggle for existence.

In the struggle for existence the instinct of self-preservation developed two mighty creative forces in man. These two forces are knowledge and imagination. The first is the ability to observe, compare and elucidate natural phenomena and the phenomena of social life; in other words, knowledge is the ability to think. In essence, imagination is also thinking; it is thinking about the world but it is mainly thinking in images, thinking in artistic form; one might say that imagination is the ability to attribute human qualities, human feelings, even human intentions to things and to the spontaneous phenomena of nature.

We read and hear of "the moaning of the wind" or that "the moon shines pensively" or that "the river whispers an ancient legend," "the forest frowned," "the water tried to move the stone," "the stone quailed under the attack but did not give way," "the chair quacked like a duck," "the boot refused to be pulled on." We say "the window panes sweated" although glass has no sweat glands.

All this makes the phenomena of nature easier to understand, so to speak, and it is called "anthropomorphism" from the Greek words anthropos—man, and morphe—form or image. Here we can see that man endows everything he sees around him with his own human qualities. He sees these qualities in everything and introduces them into everything, into all the phenomena of nature and into all the things he himself has created by his labor and by his intelligence. There are quite a lot of people who think that anthromorphism is out of place and even harmful in literature, but even these people are apt to say that "the frost bit my ears," "the sun smiled," "May has come"; they say "it started to rain" although rain has no feet, or "the weather is shocking" although natural phenomena are not subject to our moral judgment.

The basic trends or tendencies in literature are romanticism and realism. The truthful, unvarnished representation of people and their conditions of life is called realism. As for romanticism, several definitions have been given but there is as yet no accurate and fully satisfactory formula which is accepted by all historians of literature. Within the romantic school one must again distinguish two sharply divergent tendencies; passive romanticism which either attempts to reconcile people with reality by coloring it, or else attempts to divert people from reality and lure them to fruitless preoccupation with their own inner world, with thoughts about the "fatal riddle of life," about love and death, about problems which can never be solved by speculation and contemplation but only by scientific research. Active romanticism, on the other hand, attempts to strengthen man's will to live, to rouse him to rebellion against reality with all its tyranny.

But in the case of such classics of literature as Balzac, Turgenev, Tolstoy, Gogol, Leskov, Chekhov, it is difficult to define with sufficient accuracy whether they are romantics or realists. In great writers, realism and romanticism always seem to be merged. Balzac is a realist but he also wrote *La Peau de Chagrin*, a novel very far removed from realism. Turgenev also wrote things in the romantic spirit as did all other famous Russian authors from Gogol down to Chekhov and Bunin. This merging of realism and romanticism is especially characteristic of our own great writers. It is this trait which lends our literature that originality and force which is exercising such an ever more noticeable and profound influence over the literature of the whole world. The mutual relationship of romanticism and realism will be clearer if you direct your attention to the question: "Why does the desire to write arise?" There are two answers to this question: one of these has been given by a correspondent of mine, a girl of 15, the daughter of a working man. She writes in her letter:

"I am only fifteen but at this early age a gift for writing has shown itself in me, the reason for it being my poverty-stricken, wearisome existence."

It would, of course, have been more correct to say, instead of "gift for writing," "a desire to write" in order to embellish by her imagination her poverty-stricken life. A secondary question arises here: What can one write about if one lives a poverty-stricken life?"

This question has been answered by the national minorities of the Volga Basin, the Urals and Siberia. Until quite recently many of these had no written language at all and yet in the course of a dozen centuries right up to the present day they have enriched and embellished the wearisome, poverty-stricken life they lived in the primeval forests, swamps, and desert steppes of the East, and the tundras of the North with songs, fairy-tales, sagas about heroes and myths about gods; these latter products of the imagination are mostly described as "religious" but in their essence they too are works of art.

If my fifteen-year-old correspondent really has a gift for writing—which I hope with all my heart—she would probably write so-called romantic things, attempting to enrich her "poverty-stricken, wearisome" life with beautiful figments of the imagination, and she would probably represent people to be better than they are in reality. Gogol wrote *How Ivan Ivanovich Quarrelled with Ivan Nikiforovich*, *Old World Gentry*, and *Dead Souls*, but he also wrote *Taras Bulba*. In the first three he shows people with "dead souls" and this is terribly true; such people lived and still live even today; in painting them Gogol wrote as a realist.

In *Taras Bulba* he represented the Zaporozhe Cossacks as

god-fearing knights of gigantic strength, who could lift up a man on the points of their pikes, quite regardless of the fact that the wooden shaft of a pike could never take such a strain but would certainly break. In fact such Zaporozhe Cossacks never existed and Gogol's story about them is a beautiful untruth. In it, as in all other stories of the same cycle and in many others, Gogol was a romanticist; the reason for his being a romanticist was very probably that he was tired of observing the "poverty-stricken, wearisome" life of the "dead souls."

But does all that I have been saying mean that I maintain the inevitability of romanticism in literature? Yes, I do maintain this is so, but on condition that we make a very considerable addition to this romanticism.

Another correspondent, a 70-year-old worker, throws this in my teeth: "I have so many impressions that I just cannot refrain from writing."

In this case the desire to write has its origin not in the poverty of life but in its wealth, in an excess of impressions which bring about an inner urge to tell somebody about them. The overwhelming majority of my young correspondents want to write precisely because they are rich in impressions and feel that they cannot remain silent about what they have seen and experienced. Probably quite a number of realistic writers will emerge from their ranks but I think that their realism will not be entirely without a certain admixture of romanticism and this is quite inevitable and justified in an epoch of healthy spiritual upsurge such as we are now experiencing.

Thus my answer to the question "why I began to write," is this: I began to write because of the pressure on me of a "poverty-stricken, wearisome" life and because I had so many impressions that I could not refrain from writing. The first reason induced me to attempt to introduce into a "poverty-

stricken, wearisome" life such products of the imagination as The Falcon and the Hedgehog, Legend of the Burning Heart, stories of a realistic character such as Twenty-Six Men and a Girl, and The Orlovs.

From all this we may be fairly certain that in our literature we have not as yet had the sort of romanticism which advocates a creative attitude to reality, which glorifies labor and the development of the will-to-live and advocates the building-up of new forms of life and which also preaches hatred of the old world, the evil heritage of which we are now overcoming with such difficulty at the cost of so much suffering.

I cannot remember complaining about life in my youth. The people among whom I began my life complained a great deal but I noticed that they did so out of cunning; by their complaining they hoped to conceal their unwillingness to help each other and so I did my best not to imitate them. Later I very soon convinced myself that the people who liked to complain most were people with little power of resistance, people who either could not or would not work, and in general people with a taste for an easy life at the expense of others.

I have had plenty of experience of the fear of life. I now call this the Fear of the Blind. Living, as I have had occasion to tell, in extremely difficult conditions, I witnessed from early childhood the unreasonable cruelty and incomprehensible spite of people; I was amazed at the heavy burden falling on some and the prosperity of others. I saw at an early age that the nearer pious people considered themselves to God, the further they were from those who worked for them and the more merciless were the demands they made on their workpeople. In general, I saw much more of the base, seamy side of life than you do. Besides I saw it in more repulsive forms than you because what you see is the petty-bourgeois terrified by

241

the revolution and no longer very sure of his right to be what he is according to his nature, while I saw the petty-bourgeois when he was still perfectly confident that he was living a good life and that this very good and undisturbed life was solidly established for ever.

In those days I was already reading translations of foreign novels among which I stumbled upon books by such magnificent writers as Dickens and Balzac and also on the historical novels of Ainsworth, Bulwer-Lytton and Dumas. These novels told me of a people with strong wills and sharply outlined characters, people whose joys and sufferings were different and whose clashes were due to weighty conflicts of opinion. Meanwhile around me small-minded men and women lived their little lives; trivially greedy, trivially envious, trivially angry, they quarrelled or went to law because the neighbor's son threw a stone at the hen and broke its leg or smashed a pane of glass. They lost their tempers or grieved because a cake was burned or the meat was overdone or the milk had turned. They could lament for hours on end because the grocer had added a farthing to the price of a pound of sugar or the draper to the price of a yard of gingham. The little troubles of their neighbors gave them sincere pleasure which they concealed behind a simulated sympathy. I saw perfectly well that the kopek was the sun in the petty-bourgeois sky and that it was the kopek which inflamed these people's nasty, petty little squabbles. Pots and pans, samovars, carrots, chickens, pancakes, birthdays, funerals, eating until they could eat no more, drinking until they vomited and turned themselves into swine—such was the fabric of these people's lives, the people among whom I began to live. Sometimes this disgusting life produced in me a revulsion that dulled my sense and lulled me to sleep; at other times it stimulated in me a desire to rouse myself by some act of self-assertion.

Sometimes this disgust and this desire of mine found ex-

pression in some mad escapade; I would climb up on the
roofs at night and bung up the chimneys with rags and dirt.
I would throw a handful of salt into the soup boiling on
the stove or blow dust into the works of the grandfather
clock through a blow-pipe twisted out of paper. In general I
did a lot of things that are now called hooliganism. I did
them because I wanted to feel alive and I knew no other means,
could find no other means to convince myself that I was alive.
I felt as though I had lost my way in a forest, in a dense
thicket full of impenetrable undergrowth, in a bog into which
my feet sank up to the knees.

I remember one incident: a group of prisoners were being
escorted along the street in which I lived. They were coming
from a prison and going to board a steamer which was taking
them to Siberia on the Volga and the Kama. These grey men
always aroused a terrible yearning in me. Perhaps I envied
them, even though they were under guard and some of them
even in chains, because they were at least going somewhere
while I had to live like a lonely rat in a cellar in a dirty kitchen
with a brick floor. One day a large group of convicts was
marched along the street with a rattling of fetters. On one
flank nearest the pavement were two convicts chained hand
and foot; one of them, a big fellow with a black beard, eyes
like a horse, a deep red scar across his forehead and a mu-
tilated ear, was a formidable figure. I was walking along the
pavement and staring at this man when he suddenly shouted
cheerfully and in a loud voice:

"Hey, laddie, come on, come with us!"

It was as if by these words he had taken me by the hand.

I immediately ran up to him, but one of the guards swore
at me and pushed me away. Had he not pushed me I might
have followed that terrible man like a sleep-walker, followed
him precisely because he was strange, unlike the people I knew.
He was terrible, he was in chains, but he would lead me into

a different life. I long remembered that man and his good-natured cheerful voice. His figure is linked in my memory with another no less powerful impression: Somehow I got hold of a fat book the beginning of which was missing; I began to read it and understood nothing except one story about a king who offered a yeoman the rank of a nobleman but the yeoman answered the king with these verses:

> "—Let me live and die a yeoman still.
> So was my father, so must live his sonne.
> For 'tis more credite to men of base degree
> To do great deeds, than men of dignitie."

I copied these somewhat clumsy verses in my copybook and they served me for many years as a staff serves a wanderer, and perhaps also as a shield which protected me from the temptations and bad advice which came my way from the petty-bourgeoisie who were my equivalent of "fine gentlemen." Probably many young people encounter in their early life some such word which fills their young imagination with a motive power as a driving wind fills a sail.

Ten years later I learned that these verses were taken from *George-a-Green, the Pinner of Wakefield*, a comedy written in the sixteenth century by Robert Greene, a contemporary of Shakespeare, the Russian title of which was *Comedy about the Merry Archer of George Greene and Robin Hood*. I was very glad to have found this out and became even more fond of literature, ever the true friend and helper of men in their hard-working life.

You must know that at that time people like myself were lone wolves, stepchildren of society, while you, many hundreds of you, are the beloved children of a working-class which has become conscious of its strength, which has taken power, and which is rapidly learning to appreciate at its true value the useful work of individuals. In the Workers' and Peasants' Government you have a government which must and can help you to develop your abilities to the full and which is already gradually doing so.

You young people need to know that all the really valuable, permanently useful and beautiful things which humanity has produced in science, in the arts and in technology have been created by individuals working under incredibly difficult conditions amidst the profound ignorance and indifference of society, the hostile resistance of the Church, the self-seeking of the capitalists and the capricious demands of the "patrons of science and the arts." You should also remember that among the creators of culture were many simple working men such as Faraday, the famous physicist, or Edison; that the spinning machine was invented by Arkwright who was a barber; that the blacksmith Bernard Palissy was one of the greatest artists in pottery; that Shakespeare, the greatest playwright of all times, was a simple actor and so was the great Molière. Such examples could be quoted by the hundred.

And all these things were done by individuals who worked without having at their disposal the tremendous resources of knowledge and the technical facilities available in our days! How much easier have the tasks of cultural work been made here in our country, a country whose declared aim it is to liberate the people completely from irrational toil and that cynical exploitation of labor power, which creates a group of rapidly degenerating rich people and threatens the working-class with extinction.

Now I will answer the question: how I learned to write. My impressions came both directly from life and out of books. The first sort of impression one might compare with raw materials and the second with semi-manufactured goods

245

or putting it more crudely to make it plainer, in the first case I saw in front of me an ox and the second its beautifully tanned hide. I owe a great deal to foreign literature, especially to French literature.

My grandfather was harsh and a miser, but I had never seen and understood him as well as I saw and understood him after having read Balzac's novel *Eugenie Grandet*. Old Grandet, Eugenie's father, is also a miser and in general very like my grandfather except that he is less intelligent and less interesting. Compared with the Frenchman, my old Russian granddad, whom I did not like, definitely gained in stature. This did not induce me to change my attitude towards him but it was a great discovery for me that a book was capable of disclosing to me something I had never seen or noticed before about somebody I knew.

George Eliot's tedious *Middlemarch* and Auerbach's and Spielhagen's books taught me that although in the English and German provinces people lived slightly different from those of the people in Nizhni Novgorod, they did not live so very much better. They talked about the same things, about their own English and German kopeks; they too said that one should fear God and love Him but they too, like the people of my street, did not love each other in the least and especially did not love peculiar people who in one way or another were different from the majority. Although I was not looking for similarities between Russians and foreigners, but on the contrary was looking for differences, similarities were what I actually found.

My grandfather's friends, the ruined merchants, Ivan Shchurov and Yakov Kotelnikov, talked about the same things in the same way as the characters in Thackeray's celebrated *Vanity Fair*. I had learned to read from the Book of Psalms and loved the book very much because of its fine musical language. When Yakov Kotelnikov, my grandfather,

246

and in general all the old men complained to each other about their children. I remembered how King David complained to God of his son, the rebellious Absalom. It seemed to me that the old men were not speaking the truth when they told each other that people in general, and the young people in particular, were living worse lives and were getting lazier, more stupid and unmanageable and less God-fearing than they had been in the past. For the hypocritical characters in Dickens said just the same.

There was, of course, no system, or consistency in my reading, it was all a matter of chance. Victor Sergeyev, my master's brother, liked to read popular French novels by Xavier de Montépin, Gaboriau and Bouvier, and having read these authors he chanced on Russian books which ridiculed and gave hostile descriptions of the revolutionaries whom they called *Nihilists*. I also read these books and found it interesting to read about people who bore almost no resemblance to the sort of people among whom I was living, but seemed more closely related to the convict who had invited me to come for a walk with him. I did not, of course, understand what these "revolutionaries" were wanting which, of course, was the intention of the authors who painted them in the blackest colors.

By accident I somehow got hold of Pomyalovski's stories *Molotov* and *Little Man's Luck* and after Pomyalovski had shown me the "poverty and wearisomeness" of petty-bourgeois life, the beggarly happiness of the petty-bourgeois, I began to feel, as yet instinctively, that the grim Nihilists were somehow better respected than the respectable Molotov.

Foreign literature provided me with plenty of material for comparisons and aroused my admiration by the remarkable mastery with which it depicted people in such life-like and plastic fashion that I felt as if I could touch them. Besides, I always found them more active than the Russians, they talked less and did more. A genuine and profound educational influence was exercised on me as a writer by that great trio of French literature, Stendhal, Balzac and Flaubert, and I would most strongly advise beginners to read these authors; they are truly artists of genius and the greatest masters of form: Russian literature has not yet produced writers of such excellence. I read them in Russian but that did not prevent me from feeling the artistry with which these Frenchmen handled the language. After the mass of inferior stuff I had read, after Mayne-Reid, Cooper, Gustave Aimard, Ponson du Terrail, the stories of these great writers seemed to me almost miraculous.

I remember reading Flaubert's *A Simple Heart* one Whitsun evening on the roof of the shed where I had climbed up to hide from the holiday-making crowd. I was absolutely overcome by the story, I was blind and deaf; the noisy and merry holiday was veiled for me by the figure of that simple woman, the servant who had accomplished no heroic exploits and committed no crimes. It was difficult to understand why the plain, familiar words put together by a man into a story about the uninteresting life of a servant moved me so. There was some incomprehensible trick concealed here and—I am not inventing this—almost involuntarily, like a puzzled savage, I held the pages up to the light as if to find the solution of the trick somewhere between the lines.

I had read dozens of books in which mysterious and bloody crimes were described. Then I read Stendhal's Italian stories and again I could not understand how he had done it. Here was a man describing cruel people, revengeful killers—and yet I was reading his stories as though I was reading the life of the saints or hearing the *Dream of the Madonna*, the story of her wanderings through hell amongst the torments of the damned.

248

But what overwhelmed me completely was when I read in Balzac's *La Peau de Chagrin* the description of the orgy in the banker's house where about twenty people are talking all at once, creating a chaotic noise, the polyphony of which I seemed to hear. But the most important thing was that I did not merely hear, I also saw how each of them spoke, I saw their eyes, their smiles, their gestures, although Balzac had not described either the faces or the figures of the banker's guests.

In general his portrayal of people by means of words, his art of making their speech audible and giving it life, his absolute mastery of dialogue always inspired me with great admiration of Balzac and the French. Balzac's books are written in oil-colors, so to speak, and when I first saw pictures by Rubens they immediately reminded me of Balzac. When I read Dostoyevski's passionate novels I cannot but think that he owed a very great deal to this supreme master of the novel. I also liked the books of the two Goncourts, dry and precise like a pen-and-ink drawing, and Zola's grim and dark painting of life. Victor Hugo's novels made little impression on me; even *Quatre-vingt-treize* I read with indifference; the reason for this indifference I understood only after I had read Anatole France's novel *Les Dieux Ont Soif*. Stendhals's novels I read only after I had learned to hate many things and his calm tone and sceptical sarcasm greatly strengthened me in my hatred.

From all I have said about books it follows that it was from the French that I learned to write. Although this happened by chance I think that it was not a bad thing and I advise young writers to learn French in order to read the great masters in the original and learn from them the great art of the word.

It was considerably later that I came to read the classics of Russian literature: Gogol, Tolstoy, Turgenev, Gon-

249

charov, Dostoyevski and Leskov. Leskov influenced me, no doubt, by his amazing knowledge and richness of language; altogether this is an excellent writer who has a subtle and profound knowledge of all things Russian, a man who is still not appreciated at his proper value in our literature. Chekhov said that he owed him a great deal and I think Remisov could have said the same.

I point out these connections and influences in order to emphasize once more that knowledge of the history of Russian and foreign literature is an absolute necessity for a writer.

When I was about twenty years old I began to understand that I had seen, heard and experienced many things about which I ought to and indeed must tell other people. It seemed to me that I understood and felt certain things in a different way from other people. This worried me and made me restless and loquacious. Even when reading such a master as Turgenev, I sometimes thought that perhaps I might tell the stories of the heroes in A Sportsman's Sketches in a different way from Turgenev. At this time I was already regarded as an interesting story-teller and dockers, bakers, tramps, carpenters, railway-workers, "pilgrims to holy places" and, in general people among whom I was living would listen to me with attention. When I told them about books I had read I caught myself more and more often telling the stories differently, distorting what I had read, adding something to it out of my own experience. This happened because for me literature and life had merged into one; a book was the same sort of manifestation of life as a man, a book was also a living, speaking reality, and it was less a "thing" than were all other things created or to be created by man.

Intellectuals who listened to me told me:

"Write! Try to write!"

Often I felt as if drunk and was subject to fits of loquacity, a sort of wordy debauch resulting from my desire

to speak of everything that grieved or gladdened me; I wanted
to relieve myself by speaking of it. I had moments of tor-
menting tension when I had a lump in my throat like an
hysterical woman. I wanted to shout aloud that Anatoli the
glazier, my friend and a very gifted lad, would perish if no
one helped him; that Theresa the streetwalker was a good
woman and that it was an injustice that she was a prostitute
and that the students who used her did not understand this
just as they did not understand that Matitsa, the old beggar
woman, was more intelligent than Yakovleva, our bookish
young midwife.

Without telling even my close friend, the student Guri
Pletnyov, I wrote some verses about Theresa and Anatoli,
about the snow which melted in spring but did not do so
in order to drip down in a stream of dirty water from the
street into the cellar where the bakers were working; I wrote
that the Volga was a beautiful river, that the pretzelmaker
Kuzin was Judas Iscariot, and that life was a swinish and
painful business that killed the soul.

Writing verse came easy to me but I saw that my verses
were vile and I despised myself for my lack of skill and talent.
I read Pushkin, Lermontov, Nekrasov, Kurochkin's translations of Béranger, and saw perfectly well that I was not in
the least like any of these poets. I was afraid to write prose
because it seemed to me that prose was much more difficult
than verse; prose demanded especially sharp eyes, the ability
to see and observe things invisible to others, and a certain
exceptionally compact and powerful arrangement of words.
But for all that I did try to write prose as well, preferring,
however, to write rhythmical prose, because I found the
writing of ordinary prose beyond my powers. The results
of these attempts of mine were simply pitiful and ridiculous.
I wrote an enormously long poem in rhythmical prose which
I called *Song of the Old Oak*. In ten words V. G. Korolenko

251

demolished this "wooden" production root and branch. In it I had, if I remember right, put forward my ideas in connection with an article entitled *The Whirlpool of Life* (published if I am not mistaken in the scientific journal *Knowledge*) and discussing the theory of evolution. I can remember only a single sentence of the whole thing:

"I have come into the world in order not to agree"—and it seems that I really did not agree with the theory of evolution.

I think it was Nadson who said that "Our beggarly tongue is cold and contemptible" and few of our poets have not complained of the poverty of our language.

I think that these complaints of poverty relate not only to the Russian language but to human language as a whole. They are evoked by the fact that there are thoughts and feelings too elusive to be expressed in words. But if we set aside the things which are too elusive for words, the Russian language is inexhaustibly rich and is growing richer with amazing rapidity.

It may be useful to mention here that the language is created by the people. The division of a language into literary and colloquial language means that we have what one might call a "raw" language on the one hand and a language molded by master hands on the other. The first who understood this was Pushkin and he was also the first to show how to use the speech material of the people and how to mold it.

The writer is the emotional mouthpiece of his country and of his class, he is their ear, their eye and their heart; he is the voice of his time. He should know as much as possible, and the better acquainted he is with the past the better will he understand his own time, the more strongly and profoundly will he perceive the universally revolutionary character of our time and the scope of its tasks. It is necessary and even obligatory to know the history of the people; it is no less necessary to know what it thinks about social and political issues. Scholars who study ethnography and the history of culture tell us that the people's way of thinking finds expression in tales, legends, proverbs and sayings. And it is perfectly true that proverbs and sayings give a most complete and fascinating expression of how the mass of the people think.

In general, proverbs and sayings formulate with exemplary brevity the whole social and historical life-experience of the toiling people and it is imperative for a writer to study this material which will teach him to clench some words just as fingers are clenched in a fist and to unfold other words which have been tersely compressed by others—unfold them so as to reveal the dead things, hostile to the tasks of the hour, which have been concealed in them.

I have learned a great deal from proverbs or, in other words, from thinking in aphorisms.

It was this kind of live thoughts which taught me to think and to write. Such thoughts, the thoughts of houseporters, clerks, down-and-outs, and all sorts of other people, I found in books where they were clothed in other words. Thus the facts of life and literature mutually supplemented each other.

I have already spoken of the way in which masters of the word create types and characters but perhaps it may be useful to mention two interesting instances:

Goethe's *Faust* is one of the finest products of artistic creation, entirely a product of the imagination, a figment of the brain, the incarnation of thoughts in images. I read *Faust* when I was twenty years old and somewhat later I learned that two hundred years before the German Goethe, Christopher Marlowe, an Englishman, had also written

253

about *Faust;* that *Pan Tvardovski,* a Polish novel, was also a sort of *Faust,* and so was the Frenchman Paul de Musset's *Seeker After Happiness.* I also found out that the source of all books about Faust was a medieval folk-tale about a man who sold his soul to the devil because he wanted personal happiness and power over men and over the forces of nature. This tale in its turn was born out of the observation of life and work of the medieval alchemists who strove to make gold and produce an elixir of immortality. Among these people there were many honest dreamers, "fanatics of an idea," but there were also swindlers and charlatans. It was the failure of all the efforts of these people to achieve a higher power that was held up to ridicule in all the stories about the adventures of the medieval Doctor Faust whom even the devil himself could not help to achieve omniscience and immortality.

Side by side with the unhappy figure of Faust stands another character also known to every nation. In Italy he is Pulcinello, in England Punch, in Turkey Karapet, in our country Petrushka. He is the invincible hero of the puppet-show, he defeats everything and everybody; the police, the priests, even death and the devil, while he himself remains immortal. In this crude and naïve image the working people incarnated their own selves and their firm belief that in the long run it will be they who will defeat and overcome everything and everybody.

These two instances once more confirm what was said above; traditional "anonymous" works of literature, that is to say, the products of unknown people, are also subject to the law that the characteristic traits of some social group must be rendered tangible by the concentration of all these traits in a single individual member of the group. Strict observation of these laws by the writer helps him to create types. Thus did Charles de Coster create his Till Ulenspiegel, the national type of the Fleming; Romain Rolland his Burgun-

254

dian Colas Breugnon; Alphonse Daudet his Provençal Tartarin of Tarascon. A writer can only create such brilliant portraits of typical people if he has well-developed powers of observation, the ability to find similarities and spot differences, and if he is prepared to learn, to learn and to learn. Where there is no precise knowledge, guessing takes its place and of ten guesses, nine are wrong.

I do not consider myself a master capable of creating characters and types equalling in artistic merit such types and characters as Oblomov, Rudin, Bazarov, etc. But even in order to write *Foma Gordeyev* I had to observe many a dozen merchants' sons who were dissatisfied with their fathers' lives and professions. They all had a vague feeling that there was little point in their monotonous, "poor and wearisome" life. The prototypes of my Foma, doomed to a dull life, resenting it, and given to brooding, either took to drink and became debauchees, men who "burned up life," or else they became such "white ravens" as Sava Morozov. Foma Gordeyev's godfather, Mayakin, was also put together out of a lot of little traits, out of "proverbs," so to speak; but I had not been mistaken; after 1905, when the workers and peasants had paved a road to power for Mayakin with their own bodies, the Mayakins we all know played a not insignificant part in the struggle against the working-class and even now have not yet ceased to dream of returning to their old haunts.

Young people have asked me why I wrote about tramps.

Because living among the lower middle-class and seeing around me people whose only object was to exploit other people by hook or crook, to turn other people's blood and sweat into kopeks and turn the kopeks into rubles, I, like my fifteen-year-old correspondent, came to hate fiercely the parasitic life of these commonplace people who resembled each other like copper coins from the same mint.

Tramps for me were "uncommon" people, they were un-

255

common because they were "declassed," men who had cut loose from their class or had been repudiated by it and had lost the most characteristic traits of their class. In Nizhni Novgorod, in the "Millionka," among the "Golden Company," former well-to-do tradesmen, my own cousin Alexander Kashirin who was a gentle dreamer, the Italian artist Tontini, Gladkov, who had been a secondary schoolmaster, a certain Baron B., a former assistant police inspector who had done a long stretch for robbery, and the famous thief, "General Nikolka," whose real name was Vander-Vliet, all got on famously together.

In Kazan, in the "glass factory," I came across another lot of about twenty people of no less divergent origin. There was a "student" whose name was Radlov or it may have been Radunov; an old ragpicker who had done ten years' penal servitude; Vasska Grachik, a former footman of Governor Andreyevski; Rodzievich, a Byelorussian engine-driver, son of a priest; Davidov, a veterinary surgeon. Most of these people were diseased and drunkards; fights between them were frequent but ties of comradely mutual assistance were well developed among them and everything that they managed to earn or to steal they ate and drank in common. I saw that although their living conditions were worse than those of ordinary people, they considered themselves better and indeed they felt better than ordinary people because they were not greedy, they did not try to get the better of each other, they did not hoard money—

There were strange people among these tramps and there were a lot of things about them I did not understand, but I was greatly biased in their favour by the fact that they did not complain of life and spoke of the comfortable life of the respectable people sarcastically or ironically yet not out of a feeling of concealed envy, not because the grapes were sour,

256

but rather out of a feeling of pride, out of the knowledge that although they were "living badly," they were nevertheless better men than those who were "living well."

Kuvalda, the dosshouse-keeper, whom I described in *The Outcasts*, I saw for the first time when he appeared before Kolontayev, a justice of the peace. I was astounded by the dignified bearing with which this man in rags answered the questions of the justice of the peace, the contempt with which he replied to the policeman, the prosecutor and the innkeeper whom he had beaten up. No less impressed was I by the mild irony of a tramp in Odessa, who told me the story which I used for my own story, *Chelkash*. I met this man in a hospital where we were both lying ill. I well remember his smile which bared a row of magnificent white teeth, the smile with which he ended the story about the dirty trick played on him by a lad whom he had hired to do some work for him. "So I let him go and keep the money; 'Go, you fool, and fill your belly!' "

He reminded me of Dumas's "noble" heroes. We left the hospital together and as we were sitting together in a camp outside the town, he treated me to some melons and suggested: "Perhaps you'd like to come and do a good job with me? I think you'd manage all right."

I was extremely flattered by this suggestion but by that time I already knew that there were better things I could do than smuggling and thieving.

So I would say that my predilection for tramps resulted from my desire to portray "uncommon" people rather than the mean petty-bourgeois types. Of course, this was partly due to the influence of foreign, and especially French, literature, much brighter and more colorful than our Russian. But what moved me above all was the desire to embellish with my own imagination the "beggarly, wearisome life" about which my fifteen-year-old girl correspondent wrote.

257

This desire, as I have already said, is called "romanticism."

For me, there are no ideas beyond man; for me, man and only man is the creator of all things and all ideas, he is the miracle-worker and the future master of all the forces of nature. The most beautiful things in this our world are the things made by labor, made by skilled human hands, and all our thoughts, all our ideas, are born out of the process of labor, as shown by the whole history of the arts, science and technology. Thoughts come after the facts. I bow to man because beyond the incarnations of man's reason and imagination, I feel and see nothing in our world.

And if it is thought necessary to speak of sacred things, then the one sacred thing is the dissatisfaction of man with himself and his striving to be better than he is; sacred is his hatred of all the trivial rubbish which he himself has created; sacred is his desire to do away with greed, envy, crime, disease, war, and all enmity between men on earth; and sacred is his labor.

MAXIM GORKY, 1928

(*Translated by Edith Bone*)

MAXIM GORKY

A BIBLIOGRAPHY AND CHRONOLOGY

1868   Alexei Peshkov (Maxim Gorky), son of a cabinet-maker, born in Nizhni-Novgorod.

1872   Gorky's father dies.

1878   Gorky's mother dies. Gorky is sent to work as errand boy in a boot and shoe shop.

1880   Gorky serves on a river steamboat as dishwasher.

1881–1882   Gorky works as errand boy in a bookshop and as apprentice to an icon painter.

1884   In Kazan without work or money, Gorky frequents river jetties in the company of tramps. In the autumn goes to work for a pretzel maker.

1888   Carries on revolutionary propaganda in the village of Krasnovidovo on the Volga. Works as baker in Kazan and at the Caspian fisheries. Works as night watchman at the station of Dobrinka and later as goods supervisor and weighman at small railway stations.

1889   First arrest. Confined in the prison of Nizhni-Novgorod. After release, is kept under police surveillance.

Leads a wandering life along the Volga, in the Don region, the Crimea and the Caucasus.

1892   Gorky's first short story, *Makar Chudra,* is published in the Tiflis newspaper *Kavkaz.*

1893   *Emelyan Pilyai*
The Siskin That Lied and the Woodpecker That Loved the Truth

1894   *Grandfather Arkhip and Young Alec*
         Orphan Paul (Luckless Pavel)*
         My Travelling Companion
         Once in Autumn*
         A Mistake
         The Song of the Falcon*

1895   *Conclusion*
         Old Izergil
         Chelkash*
         Gorky works on the *Samara Gazette*, to which he contributes short sketches under the pseudonym Yegudiel Khlamida.

1896   Contributes sketches to the *Samara Gazette*, *Nizhni-Novgorod Page*, and the *Odessa News*. Gorky contracts pumonary tuberculosis and goes to the Crimea for his health.
         The Affair with the Clasps*
         On a Raft*

1897   *Konovalov**
         Goltva Fair
         Mischievous Lad
         The Orlovs*
         Down-and-Outs
         Malva*
         From Boredom
         My Fellow Traveler*
         The Khan and his Son*
         Boles (Her Lover)*
         Comrades*
         Heartache

------

* An asterisk marks works translated into English so for as these have come to our knowledge.

Vyvod (An Adulterous Wife; also: The Exorcism) *

Varenka Olesova *

Ex-Men (Creatures that Once Were Men; also: Outcasts, Men with Pasts) *

In the Steppe *

Zazuerina (The Green Kitten) *

Mischiefmaker (An Insolent Man) *

1898   Gorky is sent under convoy to Tiflis and imprisoned. Released under police surveillance at end of May.

First book, *Tales and Sketches,* Vols. I and II, appears.

Chums *

A Shady Character (A Rolling Stone, A Strange Companion) *

A Reader

Cain and Artem

1899   *Foma Gordeyev*

Twenty-Six Men and a Girl *

Kirilka (Waiting for the Ferry) *

Concerning the Devil

Red Vaska *

The Hungry Ones

1900   *Three* *

1901   Gorky arrested on a charge of issuing mimeographed "Criminal Appeals to the Workers of Sormovo." Released from prison on health grounds.

Song of the Stormy Petrel *

1902   Gorky exiled to Arzamas under police surveillance. Elected honorary member of the Russian Academy, but the election annulled by

263

order of Nicholas II. Forms close contacts with
active Social-Democrats.
Commonplace Folk
Lower Depths (a play)*
Smug Citizens (a play)*

1904   First volume of magazine published by the
"Znanie" Company started by Gorky, appears.
A Man
Summer Folk (a play)*

1905   Gorky is imprisoned on January 11 in Fortress
of Peter and Paul on a charge of composing a
manifesto calling for the overthrow of the ex-
isting order. Public opinion compels Tsarist
Government to release him.   .
Notes on Commonplace People
Soldiers
Prison
Children of the Sun (a play)*
Three Days
Bukoyomov
The Story of Filipp Vasilyevich
Gorky contributes to Bolshevik Paper, *Nov-
aya Zhizn* (New Life), edited by Lenin.

1906   Gorky goes to America to collect funds for the
Bolshevik Party. Addresses political meetings
in New York. Agitates in France against a
French loan to the Tsarist Government. In
October goes to live on Island of Capri.
Russian Tsar
Enemies (a play)*
City of the Yellow Devil
Magnificent France
One of the Kings of the Republic

Comrade
Pillar of Morality
Barbarians (a play) *
The Kingdom of Tedium
Mob
My Interviews
The Masters of Life
A Priest of Morals
Fair France

1907   Gorky attends the Congress of the Russian
       Social-Democratic Party in London as voting
       delegate. Forms friendship with Lenin.
       *Mother**
       January 9th

1908   Lenin visits Gorky on the Island of Capri.
       Life of an Unwanted
       Soldiers
       Cynicism
       *The Confessions**
       The Last Ones (a play)

1909   *Okurov Town*
       The Life of a Superfluous Man (The Spy) *
       Summer

1910   *Matthew Kozhemyakin* (The Life of)
       Vassa Zheleznova (a play) *
       Queer People (a play) *

1911   *Tales*
       Mordovian
       Self-Taught Writers

1912   *Tales*
       Birth of a Man
       *Italian Tales**
       *Russian Tales**

An Incident from the Life of Makar

1913 *In Old Russia*
The Master
*Childhood**
The Karamazov Spirit
Gorky returns to Russia on December 31,
Literary Editor of the magazine, *Prosvesh-chenie* (Education).

1914 *Childhood* (Conclusion)
Preface to first collection of stories by proletarian writers.

1915 First appearance of magazine *Letopis* (Chronicle), edited by Gorky.
Out in the World (Fragments)

1916 *Out in the World**

1917 Gorky founds in Petrograd "Society of Culture and Freedom."

1919 Gorky heads commission on the welfare of artists, founds World Literature Publishing House and edits "Life of the World" series.
*Recollections of Tolstoy**

1920 *Vladimir Ilyich Lenin**

1921 Gorky goes abroad in view of recurrence of pulmonary tuberculosis.

1922 *Leonid Andreyev*
V. G. Korolenko
*The Old Man (The Judge; a play)**
Queer People (a play)
The Zykovs (a play)*
Children (a play)

1923 *The Times of Korolenko**
*My Universities**

First Love*
Tale of Unrequited Love
A Watchman*
On the Harm of Philosophy*
N. E. Keronin-Petrapavlovsky
A. P. Chekhov*
Leo Tolstoy*
M. M. Kotsyubinsky
Through Russia*
The Birth of Man*
The Icebreaker*
Gubin*
Nilushka*
The Cemetery*
The Steamer*
A Woman*
In a Mountain Defile*
Kalinin*
They Are Coming
The Dead Man*
Hodgepodge
An Evening at Shamov's
An Evening at Panashkin's
An Evening at Sukmomyatkin's
Light-Grey and Light-Blue
A Book
How They Composed a Song
Bird's Sin
A Silver Ten-Kopek Piece
Happiness
A Hero
A Clown
Onlookers
Timka

A Light-Minded Man
Strasti-Mordasti
By Changul River
A Jolly Chap
A Maiden and Death (a fairy tale in verse)
A Ballad of Countess Helene de Coursi (in verse)
A Romantic
A Mordvinian Woman
A Little Girl
A Fire
A Theft
Bandits
Complaints
Tales
Fragments From My Diary*

1924   Reminiscences: Notes from a Diary*
Small Town
Fires
N. A. Bugrov
About S. A. Tolstaya
Days with Lenin*
Gorky settles in Sorrento, Italy.

1925   The Artamonovs (Decadence)*
Stories 1922-1924
The Hermit*
Karamora*
An Incident
The Rehearsal*
The Sky-Blue Life*
A Story About the Unusual
V. Lenin
Sergei Yessenin

N. F. Annensky
About Garin Mikhailovsky
The Guide
About Cockroaches
Notes of a Leader
A Story of Unrequited Love
The Story of a Hero
*The Story of a Novel**
The False Coin (a play)
Murderers
*An Emblem**

1926 *L. B. Krassin*

1927 *Life of Klim Samgin*, Part I, *The Bystander**
Journalistic articles: "Ten Years," "New and
Old," "My Greetings," "To Anonymous and
Pseudonymous Writers."

1928 *Life of Klim Samgin*, Part II, *The Magnet**
Journalistic articles: "Our Achievement,"
"Culture," "To Mechanical Citizens of the
Soviet Union," "The Red Army," "Benefits
of Literacy," "Literary Beginners," "Litera-
ture of the Peoples of the USSR."

1930 First issues of two magazines founded by
Gorky appear. *Za Rubezhom* (Foreign Lands),
Literaturnaya Uchoba (Literary Education),
also the *"Library of Novels"* Series edited by
Gorky.
Life of Klim Samgin, Part III, *Other Fires**
Stories of Heroes
*On Guard for the Soviet Union**
Journalistic articles: "Woman," "Wise Folk,"
"If the Enemy Will Not Surrender, He Must
Be Destroyed," "Humanists," "On Litera-
ture."

1931   Gorky's proposal for "A History of the Civil
War" approved. Journalistic articles: "A Hur-
ricane Destroying the Old World," "Facts of
Life," "Under the Red Banner," "To Par-
ticipants in the Civil War," "A History of
Mills and Factories," "Story of a Young
Man," On Poet's Library," "Talks on the
Craft," etc.

1932   *Yegor Bulychov* (a play)*
Journalistic articles: "On Whose Side, Masters
of Culture?" "The Old Man and the New,"
"Literary Technique," "To the Delegates to
the Anti-War Congress," "Soldiers' Ideas."
Fortieth Anniversay of Gorky's debut in literature celebrated all over USSR.

1933   *Dostigayev and Others* (a play)*
Journalistic articles: "Education in Truth,"
"Socialist Realism," "Hummocks and Peri-
ods," "Prose," "On Plays."

1934   *Soviet Literature*
Journalistic articles: "Language," "Talk to
Young People," "Proletarian Humanism,"
"Literary Curiosities," "A History of
Woman."
Gorky presides at first Soviet Writers' Con-
gress.

1935   *Culture and the People*
Journalistic articles: "The New Man," "On
Cultures," "A History of the Countryside,"
"On Tales," etc.

1936   *The Life of Klim Samgin*, Part IV, *The
Spectre*
Maxim Gorky dies on June 18.